Blaine's Way

Also by Monica Hughes

Gold Fever Trial
Crisis on Conshelf Ten
Earthdark
The Tomorrow City
The Ghost Dance Caper
Beyond the Dark River
The Keeper of the Isis Light
The Guardian of Isis
The Isis Pedlar
Ring-Rise, Ring-Set
The Beckoning Lights
The Treasure of the Long Sault
Space Trap
My Name is Paula Popowich
Devil on my Back
Sandwriter
Hunter in the Dark
The Dream Catcher

Blaine's Way

MONICA HUGHES

This title first published in Great Britain 1988 by
SEVERN HOUSE PUBLISHERS LTD of
40–42 William IV Street, London WC2N 4DF

British Library Cataloguing in Publication Data
Hughes, Monica
Blaine's way.
I. Title
823'.914 [F]   PR9199.3.H77
ISBN 0–7278–1521–0

Printed and bound in Great Britain

To my husband
with all my love and gratitude

My grateful thanks to all those who helped me in my research:

Nancy Hurn of the CNE Archives, Toronto

Joyce Pettigrew and Mary Murray of the Norwich Archives

Richard Schofield, Archivist, Scarborough Board of Education, and Bernice Thurman Hunter

Staff of the Oxford County Library and the Woodstock Public Library

Brenda Stone of the *Norwich Gazette*

Paul Moore and Marvin Hicks for settling the question of postal delivery in the 1930s

Bill Toulmin and Norman Lowe for helping clear up the confusion over the railways, and helping with timetables

To the staff of the Woodcroft Public Library, Edmonton, for their unfailing help and support

Also to John Pearce, for his insights into what I was trying to say

To the Canada Council, for an Explorations Grant which made the research and initial work on this book possible

And to Alberta Culture, the Alumni Association of the University of Alberta and the Canada Council, for funding my year as Writer-in-Residence in the English Department of the University of Alberta, during which time I was able to put all this together.

Thank you.

Monica Hughes

ONE

Susan and Gordie drove down from Toronto yesterday to show us our first great-grandchild. Susan said he's to be called Blaine after me. I must say that made me feel good clear through.

"What can I get him for a birthday present?" I asked. "Something special. Something he'll be able to keep."

Susan smiled. "I'm way ahead of you, Grandpa." She dug a small black box out of the diaper bag she'd dropped on the floor by her chair.

I turned it over in my hands. "Why, it's a tape recorder, isn't it?"

"Uh-huh. And you'll be needing these." She tossed eight or ten tapes onto the kitchen table. One slid across and I fielded it before it fell to the floor and tried to make sense of the label.

"You've got me flummoxed. Looks as if it's *you* giving *us* a present." I looked across at the wife, knitting by the stove. "We've always liked a bit of music. But this newfangled stuff..."

Susan laughed. "Don't worry, Grandpa. It's not that. In fact the tapes are empty. I'm asking you for a very special gift for little Blaine. For all of us, really, but especially Blaine. I want your memories to keep, Grandpa. What it was like when *you* were a child and growing up."

Well, I have to admit that I lay awake a good part of last night, trying to make some sense out of it all. I'm not one for dwelling on the past, not any more. But once I started in to thinking I couldn't seem to turn it off. It was like I'd built a dam across the memory of those growing up years. Now Susan and that darn machine had made a crack in the dam.

This morning I've put the first tape in, the way Susan showed me, and I'm about ready to press the two buttons that start it recording. Kind of nervous, wondering just where to begin and afraid I'll forget to use good English. I clear my throat a couple of times and turn on the machine. The tape, silently winding from spool to spool, unnerves me and I switch it off again.

Then I hear the whistle of the train near the crossing, west on the concession road, and the sound takes me back, back to that other farm down near Cornell, back to the winter of 1930...

I remember starting up in the night, wondering what had wakened me. The icy air rushing in between my long johns and the cosiness of the old feather bed. Darkness and the beating of my heart as I listened.

Sudden as a sword, light squared the window frame and leapt around the room so that one by one the battered chiffonier, the wardrobe like an upended coffin, my old brass bed, sprang into life and stayed within my eye, frozen like a photograph.

The bed shook. Noise rocked the room. I clutched my knees to my chin, my icy feet against my buttocks.

Then the light was gone and the power and the noise. There was nothing but the rhythmic clickety-clack of a night train. Clickety-clack. The rhythm matching my heart-beat. Clickety-clack.

Oh, how much I wanted to ride those trains! Night and day they hurtled along the northern boundary of our farm, taking the shortcut from Buffalo to Detroit across the southern tip of Ontario. Dad had explained their route to me and showed me their destinations on the old atlas, but the printed names were not nearly as exciting as Mom's stories about the rich ladies and gentlemen who travelled those trains. When she showed me the pictures in the old *National Geographic* her eyes lit up.

"Look at those armchairs and that silk drapery. Like a palace on wheels." Her eyes would shine and she'd look beautiful.

One day, I promised myself, I'll leave Cornell and find the real world, the world where dreams come true, where we aren't poor anymore. And I'll take Mom with me.

Every fine morning I used to trudge on my six-year-old legs up to the north boundary to watch the trains go by. I remember, one special wintry day, sitting on the fence with the wind cutting through my thin jacket. I pushed my hands into my pockets and waited, shivering. My fingers touched last week's penny, not yet spent.

In a moment I had scrambled from the top of the stump fence over the wire to the right-of-way. The rail gleamed dark and hard, and when I touched it I could feel a faint trembling in the metal. A train was coming!

I balanced my penny and scrambled back. The ground shook. Over to the west I saw a plume of black smoke. There was the train! I yelled and cheered. The black engine belched smoke and steam. There was a second's glimpse of the open firebox, the fireman's body silhouetted against the glare. The engineer, like a king, sat at the controls, his right hand lifted in a salute to me, a salute casual and yet royal. I waved and hollered back.

One-clatter. Two-clatter. Three-clatter. The railway cars swept by. Flashes of people eating, drinking, talking. A stone from the ballast between the rails spun down the slope. An eddy of wind was sucked into the emptiness behind the train. It smelt of iron and oil, of soot and bitter coal dust.

I scrambled onto the right-of-way and began to search. There was my penny, down among the ballast chips, still warm from the pressure of the steel wheels.

"Mom! Mom!" I ran all the way back to the house. "Mom, just look what I did!" I held out my penny, the king's bearded face pressed flat, the letters around the edge stretched out as if they had been written in chewing gum.

"I hope you don't think you'll get another penny after spoiling that one," Mom snapped. She pushed her hair out of her eyes and went on pounding the bread dough as if she hated it.

"I don't *want* another. I'm going to keep this one for *ever*." What was the matter? She wasn't even excited. "Mom, don't you want to know how I *did* it?"

"On the railway line, I suppose. Like all the kids. You stay off the right-of-way, Blaine Williams, or one day a train is going to come along and squash you as flat as that penny."

I went upstairs with a heavy feeling in my stomach. All the joy had gone out of the day. It was cold and grey outside and there was nothing to do but keep out of Mom's way. And I'd wasted a whole penny.

It began to snow that day and it was still snowing next morning.

"You're going to have to drive me to Cornell for supplies," Mom said.

"I'd planned to fix the harrow." Dad frowned. He hated shopping. I couldn't figure why.

"That'll keep. You'll be sorry if we're snowed in with nothing in the house."

"Hurry, then," he said and went out to the car. Mom kept him waiting fifteen minutes while she fixed her hair just right. Going out was always something special for Mom, even if it was only over to the Cornell store.

"Who's to see you?" Dad said. "It's not even a *town* any more. It's dead. So who cares about your hair?"

"I do," Mom said with her chin up.

"How can a town die?" I asked.

"When the heart goes out of the people, I guess."

I had this mental picture of all the people in Cornell walking around with hollow chests, and I kept a sharp look out when we reached the store, but I didn't see anything out of the ordinary.

Isaac Johnson was the owner. He had a handsome glass-topped gas pump right out in front, so you couldn't miss it if you were driving by, though not many people did any more. There were houses down both sides of the road, though only a few were still lived in. The schoolhouse was on the left past the store, and one family made a little extra boarding the teacher.

While Dad was hauling a hundred pound bag of flour and a bag of sugar and a twenty pound pail of lard out to the old Model T, I looked pretty sharply at the two old men sitting by Isaac Johnson's stove, telling stories and spitting. Maybe Dad had been joking about their having no hearts.

"Come on, woman," Dad yelled from the car. Mom

stopped fingering the bolts of cotton cloth and came out with a dreamy expression on her face.

Back home I crawled into the shadows under the kitchen table with a handful of raisins and the Eaton's catalogue. The catalogue was a wonderful part of the outside world, like the trains.

Dad despised the catalogue. "There's never a stroke of work done when that darn catalogue comes in the mail," I remember him shouting one day when dinner was late and he'd caught Mom with her elbows on the table, slowly turning over the pages, looking at the hats and dresses.

She had shouted right back. "Do you grudge me even a *look* at something beautiful?" and he'd slammed out of the house and gone back to the barn.

But *I* didn't despise it. I lay under the table and turned over the pages, not missing a single picture, even the dull ones of women's corsets and preserving jars. Halfway through the book I found *IT*. Long and racy with metal runners. The fastest sweetest sleigh in the whole world.

I forgot all about Mom telling me to stay out of the way. I scrambled up.

"Mom, d'you think Santa'll bring me this if I ask him? Would you write a letter for me so he'll know? Please."

"It sure is a beauty. Maybe we should ask your Dad."

"What's *he* got to do with it?"

"Oh, well, he'll ask Santa. That's what he'll do."

It was as good as a promise. I rushed into the icy parlour, which was never used, hollering at the top of my voice, and tore round and round the mahogany table, sledding down imaginary slopes.

By Christmas Eve there was a foot and more of good

snow lying over the farm like icing on a store-bought cake. I took a last look out of my window that night. The stars were hard and bright and the land black and white with no lights anywhere, because there were no houses close enough to see, and no one would be driving along the district road at that hour.

Could Santa find my house? It shouldn't be too hard. Small, with wood siding and a cedar-shingled roof, set down on a hundred acres of sandy dirt on the Springford Road, with the New York Central Railroad along its northern boundary. Yes, Santa could find the Williams place if he just followed the tracks.

There was an awful draught up the slit at the back of my long johns, so I jumped into bed and burrowed under the layers of blankets and quilts, feeling with my foot for the comforting oblong of flannel-wrapped brick hot from the oven.

Later I woke to feel the house shake. Was it Santa's sleigh, or just a night train to Detroit? Then...

"Wake up, lazybones. Porridge on the table!"

I gasped as my feet hit the icy wooden floor. I scrambled into my wool shirt, overalls and thick socks, and clattered downstairs with my bootlaces trailing. The wonderful smells of hot stove and oatmeal and toast were solid enough to touch. I took a deep sniff.

"Just look at you!" Mom knelt to do up my laces and wetted the corner of a cloth at the reservoir to rub my face and hands. "Stand still. What a mess you are. Your hair!"

The comb scraped my scalp. "Ouch! Ouch!" I tried to look round, but Mom's hand was firmly on the top of my head. I couldn't see a sleigh anywhere. Just two knobby parcels wrapped in brown paper on the table by my place.

"Presents!"

"D'you want to open them now?"

"Where's Dad?"

"In the barn. He'll be back in a minute."

"I'll wait then."

As I swallowed spoonfuls of thick grey porridge I worried. The sleigh must be somewhere. Santa wouldn't have given up just because the stove chimney was too small, would he?

Then Dad was stamping off the snow, washing his hands, coming into the kitchen in his socked feet.

"Happy Christmas, Dad!"

"Happy Christmas, son. Say, you haven't opened..."

"I was waiting for you."

I unwrapped the first parcel. In it was a scarf, of the same brown and grey I'd seen Gramma knitting with the last time we'd been up in Norwich for a visit. The second held a real Lindbergh aviator's helmet, made of leather and lined with flannel stuff. Just like the ones the big guys who went to school wore.

"Oh, boy!" I put it on. The front came down past my eyebrows and I could feel the flaps dangling on either side of my chin. "Look, Mom. Isn't it great?"

She made a funny face, like she was trying not to laugh. "You're growing so fast I bet by the time you're ready for school it'll fit you fine."

"It's fine right now." I kept it on while I finished my porridge. But where was my sleigh?

Dad tipped the last of his tea down his throat. "Well, I'm off."

He went out to the summer kitchen, leaving the door open so all the cold air rushed into the kitchen. I expected Mom to yell at him, but she didn't.

"Bless me, whatever's this behind the door? Blaine, you'd better come and see."

I slid from my place and ran. There, behind the door of the summer kitchen, was a shining varnished sleigh with bright red runners.

"For *me*?"

"Can't think who else it'd do for." Dad went out and I sat on the icy floor and ran my fingers over the smooth runners. It smelt of paint and varnish and fresh wood. It was so beautiful I could hardly bear it.

"Can I go out now, Mom?"

"You haven't eaten any bread..."

"*Please.*"

"Okay, but let's see you well wrapped up." She pushed my arms into an old sweater and then into the winter coat whose cloth was so thick I couldn't bend my elbows. My toque was jammed down over my eyebrows and the new scarf wound round my forehead and crossed over chest and tied behind. My mitts were on a cord threaded through my sleeves and I had two pairs of socks in my rubber boots.

"There you go. Have fun."

I could hardly move, but I wasn't about to complain. I held the sleigh by its new white cord and waddled out towards the barn, where the earth ramp up to the hay loft would make a super sledding place. I was sweating and out of breath by the time I had struggled through the knee-deep snow to the top of the ramp.

Then, stomach down on the sleigh, a shove off with a foot and I was flying like Lindbergh, the wind whistling past my face, the tears freezing on my cheeks and my nose dribbling into the folds of my new scarf. Like Lindbergh, or the engineer of the train ploughing through the snow on the way to the big city.

I hauled the sleigh up to the top and hurtled down again. This time I was faster and went further across the yard. Off to the top again, with my breath puffing like the train engine. One more run, faster than ever. The snow was smoothed by the runners now; if I could just stay in the tracks I had made I should be able to make it clear across the yard.

Stomach down. Fast, faster. Then a bump that jolted my teeth. The sleigh veered to the right, over towards the pile of rocks that littered the yard. I pulled frantically at the steering bar. It had jammed with a lump of snow and, as I tugged, the rope snapped in my hands. I was heading for this huge stone. I shut my eyes. Then I was flying through the air. Landing on my back with a jolt. I couldn't breathe at all. I was going to die.

"Mom!" I managed a painful wheeze, as thin as the cry of a snared rabbit. My chest hurt all the way down.

Mom ran across the yard, her apron flapping. "Blaine! Are you all right! Oh, lord, I thought you were dead!"

I tried to tell her I *was* dying, but only a painful wheeze came out. Now I know how a fish feels, I thought, gasping, before you wop it over the head. Mom picked me up and began to carry me back to the house.

"No!" I wriggled and kicked till she dropped me. "Sleigh," I managed to gasp.

"It'll keep."

But I shook my head and wouldn't move until she went back and pulled the sleigh out of the rock pile.

My beautiful sleigh! One of the runners had twisted clean underneath and the cross supports were broken off. Where the runner was bent the red paint had flaked off showing cheap white metal. Looking at it made my chest hurt even worse, but I made Mom haul it back to the house while I staggered along beside her.

Once I got my wind back Mom was in worse shape than me. She had run out in her house slippers and they were full of snow, while her cotton stockings hung in wet folds. She stripped them off, to show feet that were purple with white blotches. She had to sit by the fire and thaw them in a basin of hot water, while I crouched close to the stove with a mug of hot cocoa, stroking the runners of my broken sleigh.

When Dad came in looking for his dinner, Mom had just put on dry things and was starting the potatoes.

"What *have* you been doing, Lil? I'm hungry."

She told him the story.

"He could have been killed, Ed. If I hadn't seen it happen he'd have lain there till he froze to death."

"Tumbles are part of growing up, woman. You've got to stop babying him."

"And just look at that sleigh! Those runners are as soft as taffy, nothing but tin painted over."

"I'll take it back to Isaac and make him fix it or change it."

"You won't. You know you won't. You're just talking. You never stand up for yourself. You let people walk all over you and rob you blind. Why'd you buy such a poor thing in the first place?"

"You know fine we couldn't afford the one in the catalogue. Two dollars and fifty-nine cents! Isaac's was a quarter the price."

"Nothing for nothing. Just this once couldn't you have...?"

"Why d'you go on, woman? You know we don't have enough cash."

By the time they'd finished quarrelling the stew had burned. And that was the Christmas of 1930, the beginning of the Great Depression.

Though there was great sledding weather in the new year I had to make do with a flattened cardboard box. It wasn't much fun, and it was easier to forget about my broken sleigh when I was making snowmen or tracking down rabbits in the sugar bush at the bottom of the farm. I tried making string traps for the rabbits, but I never caught any. In that silent winter world the only sound and excitement was when the trains went by, day and night, from east and west.

Then, one morning, I woke up to a new and different sound. Plop. Plop. Plop. I jumped out of bed and yelled as my foot hit an icy puddle in the middle of the floor. The ceiling was dripping and outside the white world had dissolved into mush. The snowman under the big mulberry tree beneath my window had lost his head.

"Spring's coming," I yelled as I ran down to breakfast. "There's even spring in my bedroom. In the middle of the floor."

"Here, put this under the drip." Mom handed me a graniteware basin and I ran upstairs and placed it under the worst drip. The sound changed from a slow 'plop, plop' to a high musical 'ping, ping'. I looked up. The ceiling was a funny grey colour and it sagged in the middle like a puppy's fat tummy. I ran down to tell them about it.

Dad groaned. "Well, I've got to see to the animals." He headed for the door.

"Now you just wait up, Ed Williams. I've told you and told you about that roof. You've *got* to fix it."

"Don't you start in on me, Lil. It'll have to dry out before I can touch it."

"Will you do it *then*?"

"As soon as I can afford a load of shingles."

"You *said* that last year and the year before that!" Mom was screaming and I slumped down in my chair, as invisible as possible. "What do we do *now*? What if the whole ceiling comes down?"

But she was talking to the air. Dad slipped out the door with that stony look on his face.

"Oh!" Mom stomped her foot and glared around the kitchen as if she hated everything in it.

"Never mind, Mom." Why should she be mad when spring was here at last? I gobbled my porridge and spread honey thickly over my bread and licked the spoon tidily.

"Don't you dare put that spoon back in the pot," Mom snapped. She had eyes in the back of her head, I thought. Then she whisked out of the kitchen and I could hear her feet upstairs. When she came down her face was even fiercer. She rummaged through the kitchen drawer until she found the ice pick. Then she went out to the summer kitchen and came back with one of the big galvanized pails that was used for carrying water from the pump to the house.

"Come on, Blaine. I need your help."

"Yes, Mom." It felt good to be needed, though her fierce face sure scared me.

The bulge in the ceiling of my room was bigger than before. Mom stood a chair beneath it.

"Now hold the chair real steady." She climbed up and started hitting the ceiling with the ice pick.

"Mom, what are you *doing*? Dad'll kill you."

"I'll kill him," she said between her teeth. The ice pick suddenly went through and the drip turned to a trickle and then to a gush. She jumped down and set the pail on the chair. This was lots more fun than jumping puddles. I wondered what would happen next. The ceiling had lost most of its bulge, though it was still a funny colour and it had a jagged hole in the middle where the pick had gone through.

"Come on, Blaine. I've got to look in the attic." She ran out of the bedroom with me at her heels.

The farm had been built for a bigger family, with four upstairs bedrooms and one down. Three of the four were empty, with windows uncurtained and rolls of dust in the corners where the draught had blown them. One of the rooms was piled with battered old steamer trunks and boxes, and in the ceiling was the trapdoor to the attic.

Mom heaved one of the trunks on top of another and climbed up. I could see her legs in their beige lisle stockings waving to and fro. Then they vanished and I was alone.

I stared up. Suppose she never came down again? Suppose something horrid was up there waiting for her? There was a slithering sound and I squeaked and backed away. But it was only Mom's slippers and cotton stockings and knickers firmly elastic around the knees.

"Get all the basins and pans from the other bedrooms," she said, "and empty them into the big pail in your room. Then bring them here. I should have done this in the first place."

By the time I'd emptied all the pans and passed them up to her the big pail in my room was full to the top.

"Next plop and it'll be over."

She clicked her tongue and ran to my room and tried to push up the window. It had stuck with the damp and she had to hit the frame before she could budge it. When she got it open and had put the wooden slat in to hold it up a waft of spring air came in, sweet and wet. I took a big sniff of it.

"Blow your nose," snapped Mom. Then she heaved the big pail over to the window. It sloshed a bit as she got it up on the sill. Dad was right underneath, walking from the barn to the back porch. Mom heaved the pail over the sill. Splash, smack in front of Dad's feet.

Dad was usually a slow moving man, but that time he really jumped. Only not quite quickly enough. Mom pulled the chunk of wood out and let the window shut. She was smiling for the first time that day.

"You were a real help, son. Let's go down and get

warmed up at the stove and I'll get you a piece of bread and sugar."

It stopped raining in a couple of days and the ground dried up real fast. Then it was time for Dad to start ploughing, trudging up and down the field behind Pie and Snow, our two work horses, leaning his weight on the plough handle to force the point of the share under the soil. Stones were forever catching against the share and dulling it, so that Dad would have to take the point off and walk back from the bottom field to the shed to put a new edge on it with the grindstone.

One day it broke. I was helping Mom with the vegetables for the stew, cutting up carrots, when Dad stomped in with a face like thunder. He took the tobacco tin with the egg money in it from its place on the mantelpiece.

"Are you going to the store, Dad?" I asked. "Can I come?" But he didn't answer. He just put the money in his pocket and walked out.

"Mom, what's the matter? Why won't he...?" I looked up. Mom was staring at the door. Slowly she looked around our cosy kitchen as if she hated it, and then she looked down at herself. For just a second I saw her the way she must have seen herself, in a washed-out cotton dress and an apron made from a sugar sack, her shoes split at the sides, past mending even if we could have afforded to pay the cobbler.

A train went by, shaking the house. Mom stared out of the kitchen window, past the mulberry tree towards the tracks. "That's the real world," she said softly. "There, at the end of the line. Oh lord, how I wish..."

She leaned her head against the glass, watching the train go by. I stood beside her, counting the cars. If you could count all the cars in a freight train and get it right, you'd get your wish, Mom said. But I could only count up to twenty-five in that spring of 1931.

TWO

"It's not good for the boy to be alone so much," I overheard Gramma say to Mom once. "You should have put him in school last year."

Mom got her stony angry look and I crept away, wondering why being alone should be such a bad thing. There was so much to do.

In the spring I followed Dad as he ploughed, looking for interesting grubs and beetles. I tried to get the beetles to race each other, but the stupid things just dug back into the dirt and wouldn't play. I tried taking them back to the yard where the dirt was packed too hard for them to dig in and escape, but as soon as I got a good race started the chickens all crowded around and ate them up before I got a winner. So I caught more grubs and beetles and fed the chicks until they got real tame — the Plymouth Rocks, the White Leghorns and the funny fat Rhode Island Reds. They'd even let me hold them and stroke their dusty feathers.

In summertime, when it got too hot to play out in the yard, I'd go into the barn. It was a wonderful place, cool and high, full of mysterious shadows, out of which the pigeons swooped tantalizingly. I tried to make friends with them, but they were as stuck up as the people in Tillsonburg compared with the folks around Cornell.

The pigeons puffed their chests out importantly, their silky necks flicking busily back and forth as they searched through the straw for grains of wheat and oats. Whenever I got close enough to pet them they'd fly off, whirl around and then settle just out of reach, as if they were daring me to follow them.

One day I did just that. The roof of the barn was held up by twelve by twelve uprights, like great trees, and every dozen feet or so cross-beams ran across the width of the barn, fastened to the uprights by angled supports, like great spreading branches. From these branches the pigeons looked down and mocked me with their tilted heads and bright eyes.

"I'll show you!" I yelled, and began to climb. It wasn't very hard, because the uprights had pegs hammered into them at intervals. No harder than climbing the mulberry tree at the side of the house.

Dozens of pigeons waited for me on the first cross beam, but as soon as I reached out a hand to them they sidled coyly away. I edged along the beam with the pigeons shimmying ahead of me. By the time I'd reached the next upright most of them had flown to the beam above, twenty-four feet or so off the ground. They sat in a row with their heads tilted to one side and peered down at me out of their beady eyes. They seemed to be saying: Come up here and *then* we'll play with you.

So I climbed up to the next beam and then to the next, the pigeons always one step ahead of me, until I reached the beam that ran clear across the barn just under the sixty foot vault of the roof. Up there the air was warm and drowsy, and I found that if I sat quite still the pigeons would at last come right up to me and even run across my hand on their hard cold feet.

The barn door was pushed open. I could see a patch of yellow sunlight on the floor directly below me, a small oblong patch with a small shadow man caught within its edges. I looked down on Dad's head and shoulders. It gave me a funny feeling to see him so tiny, almost like a doll.

"Hey, Dad! See me."

He looked around. I giggled and swung my legs.

"Up here!"

His hands shaded his eyes from the slivers of light coming in through the end window, but he still didn't see me.

"No, Dad. Up on top. Can't you see me? I sure can see you."

His head tilted back so I could see his face, a small white blob. I waved and the startled pigeons flew up and whirred around. Dad's mouth opened, a small dark 'O' in his white face. But he didn't say anything. The pigeons settled down. Flies buzzed comfortably under the heat of the roof.

"What are you doing up there?" Dad's voice was kind of cracked, as if he needed a drink of water.

"Just playing with the pigeons."

"That's good. But it's time to come down now."

"Oh, Dad!"

"You come down this..." Dad stopped. I saw him rub his hands over his face. "Why, it's almost supper-time! You don't want to keep your Mom waiting for supper, do you?"

"No, sir." I scrambled along the beam to the closest upright.

"Don't...don't hurry, son. Take your time. I'll...I'll just wait for you outside." His shadow lengthened along the oblong of sunlight and vanished.

I found it was much more difficult to climb down than it had been to scramble up. I had to feel blindly for the pegs with my feet instead of reaching up for them. By the time I'd reached the ground my legs were trembling with tiredness. The pigeons peered down at me from the rafters.

"I'll be back!" I yelled up at them. "Tomorrow."

Dad was leaning against the side of the barn with his eyes shut.

"Dad?"

He grabbed me so hard by the shoulders that I thought he was mad at me. Then he squeezed me against his chest until I couldn't breathe and my face was bruised against the buckle of his overalls. I managed to wriggle free.

"What's the matter, Dad?"

"Nothing, Blaine. Come on." He led the way straight into the kitchen, where Mom was ironing, her face and neck all flushed from the stove, which was heating her flat irons.

"Give the boy something to eat, Lil."

"What? Have you gone crazy, Ed? It's not even three o'clock."

"I promised him supper. Just give him something and see he stays around the house. I'll talk to you later." He went out, leaving Mom and me staring at each other.

She shrugged. "Must be the heat. He looks kinda pale." She gave me a hunk of bread and cheese and a glass of milk, and I took them out to the shade of the mulberry tree and thought about the funny way grown-ups acted.

That evening, when real supper was over and the dishes done, Dad and I sat on the porch while he told me the story of a little boy who'd climbed up into the peak of a barn and fallen down and been killed.

"Like a jelly, he was," Dad said gravely. "Broke about every bone in his body."

I stared. This wasn't like Dad's stories of boys on

ships finding treasure islands or being hunted through the highlands of Scotland by English soldiers. *They* were exciting, but this...this was horrible. It was too real, too possible.

Next morning I went out to the barn to say good morning to the pigeons. I looked up into the shadows of the rafters. Like a jelly... The words went through my head. Every bone in his body... My eyes followed the path of a boy falling from the top beam to the hard wooden floor. SPLAT!

I shivered and ran out into the sunshine. I didn't feel like playing in the barn any more. I wandered around the side of the house. The mulberry berries were beginning to ripen. In another week or so they would start to fall softly to the ground. Then Mom would hang old sheets from the lower branches to catch them, and there would be jelly and mulberry pie.

Should I climb the tree today? Up at the top the wind would be cool and I could pretend to be in a pirate ship. I put out a hand to the rough bark. Then I changed my mind. Suppose I fell? I walked along the path to the district road, kicking up the dirt with the toes of my boots and sighing. There wasn't a train due for ages.

But I wasn't bored for long that summer. The wheat ripened early and Dad and Mom worked every daylight hour at the harvest until the field was full of stooks, each one as tall as me. Every day Dad was up at dawn, looking up at the sky, daring it to rain, as we waited for the threshing crew to come through our district.

At last word came and Dad hitched Pie and Snow to the wagon and went off to help his neighbours, as the threshing machine was hauled from farm to farm. Every evening he would come home dusted from head to foot with wheat chaff, his eyes red, too tired to eat. He'd just wash his face, pull off his shirt and pants and tumble into bed. Before I was up next day he'd have had his breakfast and left.

So Mom and I had to milk ten cows, clean out their stalls, and do all the other chores that Dad usually took care of, as well as feeding the chickens and looking after the vegetable garden. And cooking. Mom baked pie after pie and set them in the cool of the cellar against the day when the threshers would come to our place.

The days went by fast, with hardly a word between us, just work and more work, until the great day came. Dad had breakfast with us and then went out to greet the procession of horses and wagons, led by the huge threshing machine, pulled by its owner's tractor. It clattered along the rutted path from the district road, down past the sheds and the garage, to be set up at the granary end of the barn. I watched, hiding behind Dad's legs, suddenly shy at the sight of so many faces.

"Morning, Charlie."

"Morning, Ed."

"Nice day, Josh."

"If it'll just stay clear, eh, Ed?"

They all glared up at the sky. The morning mist had burned off and the sky was pearly pale. Soon the last of the dew would be off the wheat and they could start work. Only a sudden rain squall could spoil things, wasting precious time and the cost of renting the threshing machine.

Don't you dare rain, I told the cloudless sky.

The men started up the machine. It was a marvellous invention, with a long drive belt off the tractor that flapped and shook. The machine began to clatter and shudder. It was the most exciting thing I'd ever seen.

"Gee, I wish I was growed up. I want to be a farmer like Dad." I jumped up and down until Mom's hands bit into my shoulders so hard I cried out and tried to wriggle away.

"Blaine, you just listen to me," she whispered fiercely. "If you get the chance to go away once you're grown, you take it. Nobody in their right mind'd be a farmer. Nobody!" She stomped back to the house to start dinner. I could feel her fingers on my shoulders for a long time after she'd gone.

One by one the loaded wagons lurched up from the bottom end of the farm. The sheaves were hurled accurately into the flashing blades of the machine. The straw was chopped off and blown up a great pipe that led in through one of the barn windows, to fall in a golden pile inside. Before long the air was dancing with tiny silvery spikes that tickled noses and eyes.

At the other end of the machine, as if by magic, the clean creamy grain poured smoothly out, while a team of men sweated and grunted. The first man held a hundred-pound sack under the funnel, tied it off and tossed it up to the second man who heaved it on to the third, until it reached the granary, where each sack was emptied into the waiting bins and the sacks tossed down again to be refilled. Round and round, on and on, in a rhythm that did not allow a single kernel of wheat to be wasted on the hard ground.

Along the side of the threshing machine I could catch glimpses of the insides, a mass of hooked rakes, flashing blades, jolting screens, all of them hooking, slashing and raking without a moment's pause. A few of our neighbours had a finger or so missing, lost in farm machinery, so I minded what Mom said and didn't get too close.

Then she was yelling to me from the house and I had to leave the fascinating machine and run indoors. It was hot outside, but the kitchen was an oven, with pots bubbling on every square inch of stove top.

"Blaine. Take this and help me. I'll never manage alone." She pushed a potato peeler into my hand and kicked an apple box over to the sink. "Here, climb up and watch."

She flicked a peeler over the surface of a potato until it was white and smooth, and tossed it into a huge pot. "There."

It wasn't as easy as it looked, I found. After an hour my legs were fidgety from standing still and my hands were all pulpy from the water, but the potatoes going into the pot were clean, and not too small, though when I'd finished the basinful it was half full of peelings.

Mom frowned at the waste, but then she managed a tired smile.

"Good boy. Throw the peelings out for the chicks and then fix the dinner table for me. But bring me more wood first."

I ran to and fro with peelings, firewood and plates. The table looked grand when it was ready, with twenty places set around it. But the smell of cooked food was driving me mad.

"Mom, I'm starving."

"Later, dear. We'll eat later," she shouted as she rushed past me with a huge dish of steaming turnips. "Go ring the big bell. Real loud now, so the men can hear."

I rang and rang. At last one of the men turned and waved. The clatter of the threshing machine stopped suddenly and it was quiet, as if someone had flicked a switch to turn off the whole world. A cloud of golden dust hung above the barn. The men appeared from it one by one and walked slowly up towards the house.

Mom had taken the wash table from the summer kitchen and set it outside in the yard with basins and bars of Sunlight soap, so that the men could wash before coming in.

"Here, take this." Mom thrust yet another dish of mashed potatoes into my hands and sent me scurrying off.

Now the table in the big dining room, used only at threshing time, was covered with bowls of stew and dishes of mashed potatoes and turnips, boiled carrots and green beans, platters of freshly baked bread and pats of home-churned butter. Enough for fifty men, I thought, and my stomach tightened into a hungry knot.

The threshers ate in silence, their eyes on their plates, reaching out for seconds and then moving right along to pie, great wedges dripping with mulberries or slices of golden apple.

At last they finished. Chairs scraped back against the pegged wooden floor. As they filed silently out into the hot sunshine one or two nodded thanks at Mom, standing limply by the blazing stove, but most of them acted as if she weren't there. When they had gone she wiped her face with the corner of her apron and looked at the kitchen table, piled high with pots and pans, and at the dining room, where the table was stacked with dirty dishes. She let out a groan.

"Mom, can we eat *now*?"

Her shoulders lifted and she managed a smile.

"You bet. Come on, fill up a plate with whatever you want. We'll clean up the mess later."

"You mean I get to choose?"

"Sure. But don't put pie on your plate first, silly."

By the time I'd filled my plate the sweat was running down my back from the heat of the kitchen. I looked at the pile of leftovers I'd chosen and my appetite fled.

"Come on," said Mom daringly. "We'll go around and eat on the front porch. Nobody'll see us, and the devil himself wouldn't be comfortable in the house today."

After we'd eaten our picnic meal in the shade of the

west porch we went back inside and washed up pile after pile of pans and dishes, hauling water and heating it on top of the stove once the reservoir was emptied.

We had just put away the last dish in the big sideboard when a sudden rumble sent both of us running out of doors. Out of nowhere a bank of clouds had appeared. There was a shiver of suddenly chilly wind among the trees and then the rain began to pelt down.

The threshing machine's noise was stilled. In the silence I could hear the men swearing as they hauled the last filled sacks up the barn bridge and into the granary. The owner took the belts off his machine and put them in the barn to keep dry. Then they waited. Would it be only a passing shower? After half an hour it still hadn't let up and they all left, a procession of gleaming horses pulling the wagons past the house and down the road.

Dad stood by the barn looking up at the dark sky.

"Judas priest! Four hours of daylight left." He shook his fist at the clouds. "Four hours and you couldn't have waited! Another day's rent to pay on that fool machine!"

The sky cracked open with a tremendous peal of thunder and I bolted into the barn. Mom's fierce words came back to me. *Only a fool'd be a farmer*. But Dad wasn't a fool. He couldn't be. He was *Dad*.

Next day, when the fields had dried off and the crew were still threshing, I escaped for a moment from the boiling kitchen to watch a big freight go through. Dozens and dozens of cars, painted with wonderful names like New York Central, the Soo, the Chesapeake, names to spirit me away from the farm to cities where the streets were paved with gold and mothers wore silk dresses and had quiet white hands; where fathers sat behind desks and counted money and little boys had all the store-bought cake they could eat and got real sleighs out of the catalogue. So my emotions swayed to and fro between the love for our farm and the longing for the unknown.

The cars clattered and swayed. Cinders and sparks flew from the round black smoke stacks of the engines. The wind of the train's passing sucked around me as I sat on the stump fence by the right-of-way. A cinder flew into my eye. I blinked and the tears ran down my face, but I wouldn't stop counting. Fifty-two...fifty-three...I could count all the way to a hundred this year. One of these days I would count the cars right and the magic would begin: I would get my wish and travel to the big city.

The train was gone. I spat on my fingers and got the cinder out of my eye. Time to go back and help Mom. One last sniff of hot metal and oil and coal dust. And... was that wood smoke?

I looked along the line. There at the northeast corner of the farm I could see smoke and flames. Real flames that ran down the slope of dry grass and licked at the pine fence-posts and the split rails that Dad had repaired only last fall.

I ran as fast as my short legs would take me. When I got to the fire I tore off my shirt and whacked at the flames. But the flames seemed to be encouraged by the flapping shirt and one of the sleeves caught fire.

Mom'll be mad, I thought, as I dropped it and began to run towards the barn. A shirt cost money. "Fire!" I yelled as I ran, but of course nobody could hear me above the infernal noise of clattering knives and shifting screens and the hiss of the grain going into the sacks.

"Fire!" I gasped again, a stitch in my side, and ran on. By the time I'd got to the barn I couldn't say a word. I shook the arm of the closest man, Charlie Aitken from down the road a piece.

"What the devil?"

"FIRE!" Somehow I found enough breath to yell it so he could hear. He clipped off the flow of grain, tied off the sack he was holding and yelled "Sam, switch her off!" all at the same time.

In the sudden silence the men straightened their backs and looked around, dazed.

"Fire," I told them all importantly. I didn't have to be scared any more. The grown-ups would deal with it. "The fence is on fire. Over there." I pointed.

"Goddam railway," said Dad. He'd stripped off his shirt in the heat and the chaff had stuck to his fair skin and brought it out in a rash.

"Hold on, Ed. Where's your pails?"

Dad came out of his helpless anger and plunged into the dairy. Soon the men had scrambled up into the nearest empty wagon and were heading for the northeast corner of the farm, close to where the spring fed into the creek.

"Hey, wait for me, it's my fire," I yelled, but they never noticed me and I had to run all the way back to the fence, afraid of missing the excitement. By the time I got there, out of breath again and trembling with tiredness, a line of men was passing buckets along from the creek to the fence. The flames in the grass had been put out, but two rails were still alight, with hot resin bubbling out of the wood.

Pail after pail was thrown, until the flames vanished. There was a cloud of steam and then only charcoal, with a few glowing ends that the men kicked free and poured water over until long after I was sure the fire must be out.

As the wagon returned to the barn the excitement turned to exhaustion. The men's shoulders sagged and they looked as pale and floppy as unpainted jumping jacks with broken strings.

"I saw the fire," I told them.

"You did real good, boy."

"It had sixty-four cars."

"Huh?"

"The freight. Sixty-four cars."

But nobody was interested. Back at the barn Dad said, "Go ask your Mom for a pail of salted oatmeal water. We're spit dry after that."

I'd never heard of oatmeal water before. I watched Mom stir oatmeal and salt into a clean bucket of cool water. "Let me taste," I pleaded, and Mom laughed and gave me a dipper full.

"Yuch! The men'll be mad at you for sure, Mom. It's so salty."

She laughed. "You'd be surprised. Carry it down carefully, Blaine, and come right back. I've a load of work to do yet."

I tried to explain that I was much too tired after running all the way from the northeast corner and back and saving the farm from burning down, but she just turned her back and went on mashing potatoes.

Even when threshing was over Dad didn't forget about the fire. The next time section crewmen were working along the line and walked over to the house for a drink of water Dad came scowling out of the barn to talk to them.

"What about my burnt fence then? What about my fence, eh?"

The men shrugged and grinned as they handed back their glasses to Mom.

"You could always write to the company down in New York that leases the line," the foreman suggested. "But I reckon it won't do you much good. I've seen burnt fences from Niagara to Windsor. You can't expect a big railway company down in the United States to fuss about a little thing like a fence."

"Little!" I thought Dad would explode.

"If you farmers would only use metal posts and wire fences," the foreman advised as the men turned to go back to work, "and keep your grass short next to the right-of-way..." He trudged off to go on levelling the ballast between the ties.

"And where'd I get the money for posts and wire?" Dad called after him. "Or the time to cut the grass around the posts, eh?"

Poor Dad, I thought. He'd spent weeks repairing his fences, using grubbed-up tree stumps, hauled along by Pie on the stone boat. And he'd split rails, hour after hour, from the pines down in the wood lot, laid them in a zigzag course between crossed end sections, to make fences strong enough to stop our cows from wandering into the young wheat and oats.

It wasn't fair for trains to set light to fences and fields. Didn't the rich people in New York and Detroit understand what it was like to be a farmer? People in cities were supposed to be that much smarter than us, weren't they?

THREE

That year I turned seven, so when school started in the fall Dad drove me into Cornell in the wagon. I was scared and excited all at the same time, and my stomach kept doing flips. Mom had made me a new shirt out of a bleached flour sack and knickers that buttoned below the knee, cut down from an old pair of Dad's trousers. I had high socks, held up with elastic garters under the band of the knickers.

There seemed to be children everywhere in Cornell that day, girls skipping and playing hopscotch on the dirt road, boys tumbling and fighting in the grass. I clutched the honey pail with my lunch in it and wished I was still six and didn't have to go. But it was the law, Dad said.

"Down you get, son."

"But...aren't you coming in with me?"

"I've work to do. You'll be fine."

He turned the wagon and clicked to Snow to be off. In a minute I was alone, staring at the white-painted siding of the one-room school and up at the sign above the door:

S.S. no 9
1865

The bell began to ring and the boys and girls formed two lines and began to walk into the schoolhouse and there was nothing for me to do but to join the boys' line.

I'd never been inside the school before. There were six rows of desks, with an aisle down the middle, and the younger students were in front and the older ones at the back. Some of *them* looked to be as grown-up as the teacher. I was pushed into a desk in the very front row.

I wasn't so scared now, and I wriggled around to look at everything. There were so many kids. I began to count. One...two...twenty-eight! Twenty-nine including me. Even at threshing time I hadn't seen that many people all together.

"Blaine! Blaine Williams!"

Why, that was me! And everyone was staring. I blushed and turned around. The teacher was frowning at me.

"You must learn to pay attention. What *were* you doing?"

"Counting, Miss."

"Counting what, Blaine?"

"Students, Miss. There's twenty-nine."

"So there are. That's very good. But you must call me by my name." She pointed to a line of writing at the top of the board. "That is my name, Miss Wingate."

"Yes, Miss Wingate."

She gave me a smile that warmed me clear through. I watched her give the Senior First its work. She was even prettier than Mom, I decided, with shiny brown hair cut in the new short style with little wings that fell forward onto her smooth pink cheeks as she leaned over a student's desk.

I'll work like mad, I promised her secretly. I'll do anything so you'll smile at me again. I sat as quietly as I could, though the bench was cutting into the back of my thighs and my feet dangled above the floor.

Then it was the turn of the five of us in Junior First. Miss Wingate wrote letters at the top of our slates and we had to copy what she had written underneath. My hands got sweaty and the slate pencil squeaked horribly on the damp slate, but I worked on, determined to get it perfect.

At recess we all went out into the field to play baseball. We all got a chance to bat, even me. The rest of the morning went quite fast. At lunch time we took our pails outdoors and ate our egg sandwiches and apples, washed down with cold well-water, and then we lined up for the outhouses.

At the back of the schoolhouse was a long table with wash basins on it and slop pails beneath, and there was a shelf where each of us had to keep our own soap and comb and towel. One of the older girls helped me get my parting straight. (She had freckles and a squint, and her name was Marianne White. Her sister Becky was in Junior First. She had freckles too, but no squint.)

The afternoon dragged on. It was hot and flies buzzed noisily under the roof. The hard bench numbed my bottom and I had pins and needles in my toes. By the time Miss Wingate said, "You may go, students. See you tomorrow," I was feeling very peculiar indeed.

I trudged along the road after the students going west, my empty lunch pail seeming to get heavier and heavier every minute. A big boy, at least ten years old, slowed down until he was walking level with me.

"You're Mr. Williams' boy, ain't you?"

I nodded.

"I'm Jimmy Aitken. We live a piece south of you."

I nodded again and struggled to keep up with his longer stride.

"Cat got your tongue?"

I shook my head.

"Maybe you've not had enough practice talking. There's only you, isn't there? D'you know how many brothers and sisters I got? Go on, guess."

"Three," I said, thinking of the biggest family I knew, which was Mom and Uncle Bob and Aunt Rose.

"Not even close. Eight! Six older than me and two babies. Nine of us including me."

What would it be like to have brothers and sisters to play with, I wondered.

"Do you fight a lot?"

"Nah, we're on the same side, ain't we? Besides, Dad or Mom would lick us if we did."

"Don't *they* fight?"

"Course not, silly. Moms and Dads don't fight. Can't you walk a bit faster? We're getting behind."

The other Aitkens were well ahead by now, hooting and hollering, as fresh as early morning and as lively as grasshoppers. I tried to walk faster. My legs felt as fat as bolsters and my ears had begun to sing.

"Oh, Jimmy, I do feel funny," I managed to say, and then I was sitting in a heap on the ground with my head spinning, and Jimmy was yelling to his elder brother John.

They made me sit on their crossed hands and I made the rest of the trip home in style. Mom was laying the table when they staggered into the kitchen and dumped me in the old arm chair next to the stove.

"There. I knew he shouldn't have walked all that way home!" Mom exclaimed.

"Lil, he's seven years old. And he's run more miles around the farm every day for the last couple of years than the distance between here and Cornell," Dad retorted.

"Just look at him, Ed Williams. You can see he's sick. Too sick to go to school!" Mom was shouting and her cheeks were getting red.

Dad got up and shrugged into his coat. "Come on."

"Where?"

"If he's too sick for school we'll drive down to Tillsonburg and have the doctor look at him."

"Ed, that's cash money. And dinner's ready. It'll spoil."

"It'll keep fine on the back of the stove."

"I won't go." She stomped her foot. I huddled in the corner of the old armchair, wishing she wouldn't. John and Jimmy stood by the door, open-mouthed.

"Then I'll take him myself."

'Don't you dare! He's my son."

"And mine. Come on, Blaine. Lil, if you're coming, we're leaving this minute. No playing with your hair or changing your dress. Wait up, John. I'll give you and Jimmy a lift down the road."

"Much obliged, Mr. Williams."

I could see John and Jimmy eyeing Mom and Dad, who sat side by side on the front seat of the old Ford with me wedged in between them, neither of them saying a word, and the air cold enough to make icicles.

The Tillsonburg doctor was at his dinner and not pleased to be interrupted. He felt my face and looked at my eyes and tongue with a frown. Then he ran his hands down my legs and suddenly began to laugh.

"Let's get those boots and socks off, lad," he said to me.

My ankles were as puffy as bread dough and looked terrible, but they made the doctor laugh even harder. He dangled the garters that had held up my socks under Mom's nose.

"There's the sickness, Mrs. Williams. Those garters are so blamed tight they've cut off the circulation clean up to the boy's brain. If you'd left them on much longer his toes would have started to drop off like ripe berries." He pulled my toes, just to prove to me that they weren't going to drop off yet.

"Throw the stupid things away, Mrs. Williams, and let the boy go to school in overalls, for heaven's sake. The fuss you women make about school you'd think it was an invite to Buckingham Palace."

Bright spots flamed in the centre of Mom's cheeks. Her lips were pressed together as she pushed my feet back into my socks and boots and dragged me out to the car with the laces still trailing. Then she got into the back seat and pulled me after her.

We didn't say a single word as we waited for Dad. I thought he'd be even madder than Mom because of the money, but to my surprise he was whistling as he came down the walk. He started the car with a single swing of the crank and jumped in with a grin on his face.

"It's okay, Mom." I patted her hand. "He's not mad."

"Oh, hush up!" She pulled her hand away.

Dad started to sing 'Redwing,' one of his favourites.

"Do you have to?" Mom snapped.

"Well, I'd sooner sing than weep."

"I'm sure I don't know what you mean."

"A whole dollar to find out my son's garters were too blamed tight, all I had. He was asking two bucks! But Lil, you should have seen your face! So I'd sooner laugh."

"Shut up, Ed Williams. And if you tell a living soul — you too, Blaine — if you ever tell..."

"What'll you do, my Lil?" Dad teased.

"I'll...I'll leave you. I swear I will."

I scrunched hard up against her, before she could push me away. "Mom, I'll never tell, honest. Cross my heart and hope to die. Please don't leave us."

Her arm came around me and I felt her lips touch the top of my head. "It's all right, Blaine. I didn't mean it. I won't ever leave you."

When the weather began to get snappy Dad took his turn with the other fathers to bring in a wagonload of firewood and kindling for the school, split and cut into lengths for the stove. Miss Wingate was always there before eight to light the stove and sweep out the school and wash the blackboards. It was nice to arrive on a sparkling winter day and go into the warm schoolroom.

The older boys had the chore of keeping the wood-box filled and the stove going. When the wind howled through the cracks of the clapboard building they stoked the fire until the stove pipe glowed cherry red and the windows ran with moisture. Then, as the days grew shorter, we were let out of school at three so that we'd all be home before dark.

Suddenly it was Christmas time and the whole school worked on the play. I got to be a shepherd with a potato sack tunic. Becky and Marianne White were angels, their hair washed with Sunlight so it stood out around their heads like haloes. They had flour sack costumes, the company emblem still faintly visible across their fronts and at the back where the wings were fastened. Sally McIver was the mother of Jesus in a veil that was really the glass curtain from the front door of the McIver house. Everyone came, and when the play was over we sang carols and had hot cocoa and popcorn.

Christmas day came and went. I got a grey wool sweater from Gramma and a wooden pencil case with a special place to keep an eraser. Mom and Dad didn't say much all day.

Then it was 1932 and the neighbours said "Happy New Year" to each other, and "This year's bound to be better than last, eh?"

The depression didn't seem to get better at all, but we

hung on. The crops weren't bad, and in the fall I was promoted into Junior Second. After *that* Christmas we had a cold snap that lasted right through January.

The big boys and girls made a huge snowman. They let Joe and Tod and Rosemary and Becky and me help, and we had a snowball fight. I got Becky in the face and she cried and said she'd tell Miss Wingate if I didn't kiss it better. I said "Yucch!" and she cried even harder. But she didn't tell and next day we were friends again.

One day, early in February, it got a bit warmer and a few snowflakes drifted down and stuck to our coats as we went into school. Halfway through the morning Sam Baker held up his hand to be excused, stamped into his boots and went out to the outhouse.

Miss Wingate had just begun to read to us from *Treasure Island*, with the lights on because it was getting dark outside. When the door crashed open everyone jumped and some of the girls screamed. Miss Wingate looked up and the book fell out of her hands.

There stood Sam, so thickly covered with snow he looked like a snowman.

"Oh, jeez," he sobbed.

"Sam, don't swear." Miss Wingate picked up her book and placed it on her desk. "Come over to the stove. One of you boys, shut the door."

Sam moved stiffly into the room. We began to giggle. Then we saw that it wasn't just snow on his face, but frozen tears. The giggles stopped. Sam was nearly thirteen. Big boys don't cry unless something awful bad is happening.

Miss Wingate helped him out of his coat and boots and wrung a towel out in the warm water on the stove, to hold against his frozen face. She filled a basin and had him put his feet in it. We all sat in silence, staring at Sam's blue toes.

As Miss Wingate was draping a blanket over Sam's head and shoulders Tom McIver came up.

"Miss Wingate, it's drifting real hard. More than knee-deep already, I guess. And dark as the middle of the night."

"Would it be too late to send them home?"

"Jeez, they'd never find the road."

"I fell," Sam interrupted. His voice was small and tight. "I fell in a dumb drift. When I got up I couldn't see the school."

"And we had the lights on. Oh, Sam!"

"It was like my head was inside a feather pillow, honest, Miss Wingate. I thought I was going to die." His voice suddenly wobbled and I felt myself trembling inside. Was this going to be the end of the world? I didn't want to be away from Mom and Dad if it was. Next to me Becky began to sniffle.

"Hush, everyone. We're going to be just fine. We all have our lunches, so we won't starve. The firewood's getting a little low, so I'll ask the big boys to bring more in from the pile, all you can carry on one trip. Has anyone got any binder twine?"

Half a dozen hands went up. Miss Wingate fastened all the lengths together and tied one end to the latch of the outer door. "Tom, you tie the other end to your coat belt. The rest of you stay behind Tom and be sure not to let go of the string."

Once the wood pile was renewed we all settled down again and Miss Wingate went on reading. Even Sam forgot his terror and let the blanket slip from his shoulders, as he sat open-mouthed.

"...far away in the marsh there arose, all of a sudden, a sound like a cry of anger, then another on the back of it; and then, one horrid, long-drawn scream. The rocks of the Spy-glass re-echoed it a score of times..."

We shivered happily. The stove pipe glowed red. The windows creaked against the wind. Miss Wingate read on until her voice suddenly broke. She coughed and looked at her watch. "Oh, my! Past lunchtime! Fetch your pails to your desks quietly, children."

I waved my hand frantically. "Please, Miss Wingate, I got to go."

"Me too."

"And me."

"Oh, dear. I wonder if we could rig a guideline to the outhouses?"

"No way, Miss Wingate. We couldn't hardly see the woodpile."

"Very well. Boys, you will go outside. Two at a time please. And do *not* wander away from the side of the porch. And I will thank you to remember that we are not setting a precedent."

"What's a precedent?"

"You know, stupid, like President Roosevelt."

"Hah-hah!"

"Hush, boys. Tom, do you know what 'precedent' means?"

"Yes, Miss Wingate. It means we're not to get in the habit of pissing against the school porch."

The big boys roared. Miss Wingate went pink and the girls giggled. Suddenly it wasn't that scary any more.

"But what about *us*?" asked Becky. She'd been fidgeting in her desk next to me for the last while.

"We'll manage with a honey pail on the porch, with the inner door closed. *After* all the boys have returned to their desks."

We ate our lunch, and all through the afternoon Miss Wingate read *Treasure Island*. Now it was really dark outside, and once or twice I saw Miss Wingate sneak a look at the watch she wore pinned to the front of her shirt.

Then, suddenly, there was a thump against the schoolhouse wall and the sound of men's voices. Everyone's head jerked up and around as if they were all fastened to the same piece of string. Miss Wingate put down her book. She smiled, and I realized that she'd been scared too, just as scared as we were.

"Pay attention, students. I'm going to set homework for all of you." There was a groan. "Goodness knows when school will open again, and we mustn't get behind."

We were all waiting, in our coats and mufflers and rubber boots, when at last the porch door was opened. It was like a magic world outside. A white passage, its edges gold in the lamplight. Up above the sky was black and thick with stars.

The snow passage led up to higher ground, where the snow hadn't drifted so deeply. Cutters were waiting there, hung with lanterns, the lights haloed in the horses' steaming breath. We were packed in, like plums in a mason jar, and wrapped in blankets. Mr. Aitken took those of us going west and south, and Mr. McIver and Mr. Thompson and Mr. Jenkins took the rest.

The new snow glowed in the starlight. There was no sound except the bells on the harness of the horses and the singing sound of the cutter rails over the snow. I fell asleep before we got home and woke in a muddle, being lifted out and into the familiar kitchen, dazzlingly bright in the lamplight, with the stove blazing and stew and hot biscuits ready on the table.

The county plough wasn't able to get around to clearing the district road and the road into Cornell for almost a week, so Mom made me read from my primer every day, and do sums and writing on scraps of paper she found for me. Every morning I'd look out at the blanket of snow. It covered even the new telephone lines and hydro poles that had gone up last fall.

Only the railway line was clear, a dark line ruled across the white page of the countryside. A snow-plough engine had been through right after the storm, huffing and puffing and pushing the drifts aside as if they were nothing. For the trains had to go through. I'll ride them one day, I promised myself. One day.

There were no more storms, and March came in with sunny days and frosty nights, perfect to make the sap rise, Dad said, as he began to make his rounds of the sugar bush at the bottom of our place.

There was a knack to drilling the holes in the maples, he told me. They had to be slanted at just the right angle and go in deep enough but not too deep. He always spaced the holes a spread handspan from the scars of last year's taps. Dad was never greedy and he got the best high quality yield of any farmer in Oxford county.

Hammering in the spiles had to be done very carefully too. It was easy enough to break a point and ruin the hole. Last of all he hung the pails, one over each hollow spile, with a lid suspended above to stop junk falling in and dirtying the sap.

By the time the sun had any warmth in it you could hear the sap dripping as soon as you got near the bush, a slow high *plink, plink*. By the time I got home from school Dad would be going slowly around the trees, emptying the buckets into a five gallon pail, checking the flow, and maybe tapping a spile a mite deeper if the flow wasn't just right.

After a week there were enough five gallon pails full

of sap to fill the evaporator pans Dad had made. "Let me help," I begged, but it was one job that Dad really liked to do alone, slow and careful. Once he had a hard-wood fire going under the evaporator pans he never let it go out until the syrup had come. Gradually the sap concentrated and turned from watery to pale yellow to a clear warm gold like the lump of amber Mom had on a chain. He stayed up all night if he had to, tending the fire, just cat-napping and never letting the fire cool down.

Once the syrup was ready Mom and Dad filled all the jars they'd collected through the years. Then the pans were cleaned and filled with fresh sap and the whole thing started over again. I loved sugaring off. The smell of woodsmoke and syrup hung so heavily in the air you could taste it. And there was more; as Dad finished each run and scraped the pans clean he threw the remains in the clean snow to make taffy. I ate maple taffy until I felt sick and couldn't finish my supper.

"It's been a good run," Dad said at the end of six weeks. His eyes were rimmed with red from smoke and lack of sleep, but there was a grin on his lean face. "That'll bring in our tax money and a bit left over. Is there anything you need, Lil?"

"Need?" Mom looked round the patched and shabby kitchen and down at her split shoes and flour sack apron. "Well, maybe new shoes and a cotton dress, Ed. That'd be good."

Dad packed the jars carefully in the old Ford and headed off to Tillsonburg, while Mom and I stood on the porch to wave goodbye. I hated to see all those glorious golden jars go, but I knew that every bottle sold was that much cash money in the house. I swallowed spit and wished I'd saved some of the taffy.

Dad was back after dark with the car almost as full as

when he'd left. "I went to every store in Tillsonburg."

"I don't understand, Ed. It's the best quality. Yours was always the best."

"I guess the folks down Tillsonburg way don't have spare cash for extras either. Not even for my maple syrup."

"What are we going to *do*?"

"I'll drive around the neighbourhood and into Norwich; maybe sell a few jars that way. And Isaac will let us have flour and fat in trade. We won't starve."

"But it's cash we need, Ed. Tax money."

The wounds left by the spiles in the maple trees healed over. The ground dried out and the grass grew tall. At recess we made dandelion chains, Tod and Joe and Rosemary and Becky and me. Jimmy Aitken gave me a boat he'd whittled out of a piece of wood, and we floated it in the ditch next to the school field, among the frog spawn and water boatmen. The days were so full I didn't have time to worry about our having no tax money. We ate an awful lot of pancakes and syrup that spring, though.

As the days grew warmer, filled with the shimmer of grasshoppers, the school became hot and stuffy and we couldn't help fidgetting in our desks and longing for recess. I was in love with Grace McIver that summer. She was in Junior Second and had tight fair braids on each side of her round face. I walked her home from school every day, carrying her books. I never said a word, just walked alongside her and carried her books.

The 17th of May was my birthday, and when I got to school my name was written on the board in coloured chalks, and Miss Wingate had all the students sing "Happy Birthday." There were sugar cookies, that she'd baked at recess, and for me a small oblong parcel. Inside was a copy of *Treasure Island*, a little shabby, with my name on the fly leaf. "To Blaine Williams on the occasion of his ninth birthday, from Lucinda Wingate."

My very own book, that would always remind me of the day of the blizzard and Miss Wingate reading steadily on in spite of all our fears. I ran all the way home.

"Look, Dad! See, Mom! But how did she know?"

"Very nice, son," said Dad and went out to the barn.

"Your birthday's in the school register. All she had to do was look it up." Mom's voice was sharp and her hands trembled. She turned back to the stove and went on mashing potatoes for supper, while I stood hugging my precious book, blue with gold around the edges of the pages, wondering what I'd done wrong.

It was about that time that Mom started nagging Dad again.

"Why don't you drive into Tillsonburg and sell some of our eggs?"

"Nope."

"We've got to get money from somewhere."

"Nobody's buying in Tillsonburg. I can't waste the gas."

"Then hitch up Snow and go in the wagon."

Dad didn't answer. When he did that Mom got even madder.

"...all that syrup nobody'd buy. There must have been something wrong with it. Maybe you had the fire too hot." She was shouting, and I could feel my insides get tight and anxious. *Oh, Mom, don't*! She knew the syrup had been perfect, the best Dad had ever made.

"I must have been out of my mind when I married you," she went on. "To think I could have had Tim Hardy. I'd have been a bank manager's wife this moment. Or Ralph Thompson. He's got the biggest hardware store in Woodstock. But I had to go and pick a farmer..."

I put my hands over my ears.

Dad went out to go on mowing the hay.

"Sure, off you go," screamed Mom. "And I've got the vegetables and the chickens and the cleaning and the meals. Not even a hired hand."

"I'll help, Mom. I'll do more than just the eggs and feeding the chicks. I'll help with the haying," I promised. I'd have done anything to stop her being angry.

But they got the hay in while I was in school. It was really a three-person job, but Dad and Mom managed it somehow. They weren't talking when I got home from school, but maybe that was because they were so tired. But the hay was in the barn and we were safe — for the moment.

Miss Wingate had a beau that summer, and he used to drive her in his buggy to visit the farms and talk to our moms and dads.

"Blaine's doing very well," I overheard her say on a Sunday visit to our house. "He'll go far."

I raced out of the house, bursting with excitement. I'll go far. Buffalo and New York. Detroit and Chicago. I will, I promised myself, as I sat on the fence next to the right-of-way and kicked my heels against the post. *I will!*

It was a perfect summer. The wheat swelled and ripened. Every day Dad was up at sunrise staring at the sky, willing it to remain clear. "Not long now, Lil," he said every breakfast. "A couple more weeks and we'll be able to pay our taxes. We'll be in the clear."

Then, a few days before the threshing crews were due to come through, the perfect summer broke in a hailstorm that filled the ditches with white and flattened the grain with a giant's careless hand.

"You could scythe it, couldn't you?" Mom asked as we went out to look at the damage. "Maybe save half of it, lifting and scything? We could ask my dad to help us out. You know he would if you'd only ask. And Bob and his friends would be glad to lend a hand."

Dad just stood, with a face like iron, staring over his ruined fields.

"Ed, answer me. Will you at least *ask* Dad for help?"

"Nope."

"Then we'll lose everything. The taxes are due. If we can't sell any wheat we'll have nothing left to get us through the winter. All we've got is the hay for the cattle. You and your fool pride!"

"What else have I got? D'you know what this wheat'll fetch, if I could get it out, which I can't? Forty cents a bushel. It might as well lie there."

"But what's to become of us? Ed, answer me."

Dad shrugged and walked back to the house. I could feel panic knotting my stomach. What *was* to become of us? Why hadn't Dad told us? He was in charge.

Next Saturday Dad took the wagon into Tillsonburg.

"Let me go with you," I pleaded. "Please." But he shook his head and drove off without another word, leaving me with an equally silent Mom.

He got back late, just before supper. "I found a buyer for the cows," he said.

I saw the flash of hope in Mom's eyes. "We could hang on another year then. Next year things are bound to be better."

Dad went on as if he hadn't heard her. "Sam Gage'll be over two weeks Saturday. We were lucky to get him. The best auctioneer around."

"You're going to sell us out? Everything? Oh, Ed, you can't."

"You always hated farming, Lil. Why do you want to hang on now?"

"The shame of it. Oh, what's to become of us?" She sat down suddenly at the kitchen table.

I crouched in the corner by the window, my eyes going from face to face. Though I didn't understand what was happening, I knew that my orderly world was coming to an end.

"I went up to Norwich after and talked with Mr. Cameron."

"You went to see *Dad*?" Mom stared.

"He says he'll be glad of an extra pair of hands. He's not so young. And they've more space in that house than they know what to do with."

"What about *me*?" Mom jumped to her feet. "Did you stop for a moment and think how I'd feel going back to my own home that I left when I married you? It'll be like before I left. Having to wheedle every penny out of Mom. Not having my own kitchen. Having Grandmother after me every moment. Oh, Ed, I know without you even telling me that you'll never stick up for yourself and ask Dad for an honest day's wage. And I'll have Rose looking down on me, feeling sorry for me. I married you to get away from them. I won't go back. I just won't."

"Do we have any choice, Lil?" Dad's voice was gentle.

"You could have asked Dad for help any time in these last two years. That'd have made some sense. Maybe we could have hung on and made a go of it. But you were too proud. Too damn proud. And yet you're asking for his help *now*. It makes no sense at all."

"I'm asking Mr. Cameron for a job, not for charity," was all Dad said then, or ever.

Mom glared at him. For a moment my throat choked with terror. Maybe she'll up and leave for Toronto, the way she'd threatened to do more than once after a row.

Her lips got tight and ugly, but she just turned away and went on getting supper.

In the next two weeks she turned the house upside down, washing and packing, and polishing all the furniture that was going to be put up for auction. Dad spent most of his time out in the barn, but when I went out to keep him company he didn't seem to want me, so I got dragged into helping Mom. It was worse than spring cleaning, especially since Mom wouldn't talk to Dad all that time.

Auction Saturday came. Everyone was there, neighbours and strangers alike. Auctions had always been considered good free entertainment when no one could afford any other, but I sure didn't like the feeling of being part of the entertainment. Almost everything we owned was on the block: the plough, the wagon, the cutter, the butter churn and the big copper where Mom had boiled the clothes on wash days. The weather was fine, so Mr. Gage had Dad drag all the furniture out into the front yard. He said it would go better there.

There was the delicate desk from the unused front parlour, and Mom and Dad's big bed. The wash stand with the ewer and jug and two matching chamber pots with a country scene in pinky mauve. The kitchen table, scoured white with a thousand scrubbings, under which I had played caves and pirate ships.

I bit my lip so as not to cry, but when I saw the look on Dad's face as they started bidding on his old rocker I had to run off and hide in the barn. It was unchanged and still felt safe. There was the sweet hay and the smell of the sun and the drowsiness of bees and pigeons. Faintly, through the familiar comforting sounds, I could hear the woodpecker voice of Sam Gage.

"What am I offered for this fine wash tub, filled with useful kitchenware? A job lot, finder's keepers. Take a chance. You can't lose. Ten cents? Come on. You can do better than that. Thirty? The wash tub alone's worth more than that... Gone to Mrs. Aitken for fifty-five cents."

I buried my face in the hay. Everything gone. The creek and the sugar bush. My view of the mulberry tree. And the railway.

What'll it be like living at Grandpa's? I wondered. "Alistair's as tough as Aberdeen granite," I'd heard a man say about him. "The devil himself couldn't best him. Yep, if ever a man could walk up to the gates of hell and laugh at death's teeth, that man is Alistair Cameron."

I didn't know much about the gates of hell, but I sure knew what death's teeth were like. Once, when I was small, Dad had turned up the skull of a horse with his plough. Huge yellow teeth in a jaw longer than my arm. Grandpa could laugh at something like that, Grandpa could. I began to feel comforted. I rolled over on my back and stared up into the peak of the barn. After all, there would still be school and all my friends. Miss Wingate. And I could still carry Grace McIver's books home.

I fell asleep in the hay. When I woke up it was quiet outside and my feet echoed on the hollow wooden floor. Outside the sun was low, slanting gold through the dust that the buggies had stirred up in our lane and along the district road. Dad was just settling up with Mr. Gage. I knew that the auctioneer was paid a percentage of whatever the sale raised, and I could tell by his face that it had hardly been worth driving out from Tillsonburg for *this* one. Some of the stuff hadn't sold at all and was standing out in the yard looking lonely and out of place. Mom was trying to drag a chair up the porch steps.

"Now hold on there," yelled Dad, as Mr. Gage counted out dimes and quarters. "You'll strain something. It's not about to rain, woman."

"I won't have it out here a minute longer than I have to, advertising our shame."

Mr. Gage cleared his dusty throat and spat. "No shame, ma'am. The depression, that's all it is."

"Damn and blast the depression." Mom dropped the chair and stomped into the house.

I stood in the middle of the yard, feeling lost. Already it felt as if the house had rejected us, as if it knew that we'd given up on it.

"Blaine, come in and help me lift these boxes," Mom yelled, and I had to go and help load clothes, and the few oddments Mom had packed, into the car. By the time we'd finished that, Mr. Gage had left and Dad had hauled the unsold furniture back inside and begun nailing the shutters across the windows. No one had offered to buy the place. No one wanted a farm that was a proven failure, not in these tight times.

"We'll save up," Dad muttered, half to himself, half to comfort me. "Maybe things'll get better soon and we'll be able to afford to pay the back taxes. Yup, you'll see."

Mom's lips tightened when she heard him. She whisked back into the house, the tip of her nose red.

"Dad, how far's it to Grandpa's? I'm *starving*."

"It's a mite over ten miles north, son. Near by Norwich. Here, hold this rope for me."

I ignored the rope and stared at him.

"Ten miles? Dad, how am I going to get to school? I can't walk ten miles!"

Dad laughed. "That's all right, son. Don't worry about it. You'll be going to public school in Norwich. A real proper town school."

"You mean I'm not going to go back to Miss Wingate's? I'm not going to be with all my friends? Dad, you never *told* me. I won't go. I hate you! I hate you!"

With hot angry tears jumping out of my eyes I ran across the yard and the field to the back end. There I threw myself down on the ground and howled my misery. A train roared by, shaking the ground, but I didn't look up. I knew it wouldn't stop for me. It was all a cheat. The trains would never stop for the likes of us, for life's failures. I knew that nothing was going to get better. That was just grown-up words. It was all going to get worse and worse and worse.

FOUR

I had sobbed myself into silence and was lying there, my shoulders still shaking as I tried to get my breath, when two hard hands grabbed me by the waist, tossed me in the air and then dumped me back in the clover. I sat up, scrubbed my wet face on my shirtsleeve and stared. Two bright blue eyes, set in a face as scarred and weathered as an ancient tree, twinkled down at me.

"Grandpa!" I scrambled to my feet.

"What's all this malarky about not wanting to live with me?"

"It's not that. It's..." I stammered. Next to Grandpa I felt like a nothing, even though I was already almost as tall as he was. "T'aint nothing."

"Glad to hear it." He gave me a smack on the back that made me stagger. "Come on then. Get the lead out. Tomorrow's for lazybones, you know. Have you finished all that crying now? It's too late for rain and the salt'll kill the crops."

I managed a watery chuckle and strode along beside Grandpa.

"You'n me'll go ahead in my wagon and warn your Gramma to get supper on the table. Boiled chicken and dumplings, I believe she said. And pie. Your Ma'n Pa'll be along in their car. You better now?"

"Sure am." I scrambled up onto the wagon seat with a boost from Grandpa that nearly sent me flying out the far side. His horses were harnessed in the wagon, but Pie and Snow were hitched to the tail. "Are they coming too?"

"Yep. I can always use a pair of good horses. They'll earn their keep."

Comforted, I snuggled up to Grandpa's side. He clicked his tongue and the horses moved forward. As we turned I saw the house, its shutters nailed tight, the chimney cold. Blown straw littered the yard and broken rusty pieces of equipment lay like brown skeletons in the nettles by the barn.

"See you!" I yelled as loud as I could. Dad lifted a silent hand in reply; but it wasn't to him that I had called. I was saying goodbye to the house, the mulberry tree, the railway.

As we bumped over the double tracks of the crossing I bit my tongue. "Ow!"

"Hold tight, young 'un."

I twisted round to see the last of the railway. No more luck earned counting freight cars. No more dreams of New York and Chicago. *No way out.* That was something Mom used to say. Now I knew what it meant. When the road curved and the railway line was out of sight it was like a door slamming.

"If you wriggle around like that you'll fall off," said Grandpa. "And *I* won't catch you."

"Why won't you?"

" 'Cause I'm busy minding the horses, that's why."

That was an interesting point of view, very different from Mom's fussing. Maybe it was going to be all right at Grandpa's after all. If only....

"No more railway," I told him, wondering if he would understand.

"It's special or something?"

It was hard to find the right words for the dream that Mom had given me.

"They go to New York and big places like that where everyone's got enough money. Mom says..."

Grandpa whipped the horses up a slight rise, though they were doing just fine by themselves.

"Your Ma told you this?"

"She sure did. One day I'm going to get on that train, Grandpa. And I'll go to the city and earn a whole heap of money, enough to buy everything in the catalogue. Well, I *was* going to, before we moved." I sighed.

"Ah!"

We rode on for a while in silence, the wagon grinding slowly up the hills and bumping down the dips, Pie and Snow trotting along behind, happy not to be doing the pulling.

"That train," said Grandpa at last. "It don't ever stop at Cornell, do it? So it never was your train, not really. Gold and fine clothes and city life. All a kind of dream really."

"I suppose. But Mom said if I counted..."

"Your Ma's a dreamer, boy. Always was. You've got to make allowances. Oh, don't push your lip out that way or you'll trip over it! I've got the right to talk about her that way. Haven't I knowed her since she was a squealing brat, all wrinkles and red gums."

My Mom. It was hard to believe.

"You really are Mom's Dad?"

"Yup."

Parents and children and growing old. It made me feel quite funny to think about, so I stopped thinking and began to look around. The road was shaded by huge elms. Set back from it were farms with doors and shutters nailed tight, some with shingles blown off the roof, so they looked even sadder and more neglected than the others.

But there were cheerful farms along the road too,

with lines of Holsteins meekly following each other to the barn for milking. There were farms with wheat stooked in the fields and old straw piled high outside the barn.

Why didn't Dad have a neat farm with fat cows and a big extra straw pile and cords of wood ramparted alongside the house?

"Is Dad no good?" I asked. "Is *that* why we've sold up? Why we're living with you?"

Grandpa twitched the reins.

"Nope. Your Dad's a good man and don't you ever forget that. I wouldn't go so far as to say he was the best farmer in Oxford county, but he's a good man in spite of it." He stirred up the horses and looked down at me with that familiar twinkle in his bright blue eyes. "Say, I've just thought of something. You've got no call to miss that old railroad of yours. We've got a better one, with more stories about it than you'll ever hear about the New York Central."

"What's it called?"

"Well, I don't rightly know its real name, but hereabouts it's known as the Toonerville Trolley. And sometimes folks call it the Grim Reaper."

"Why? Grandpa, tell me why."

"I reckon it's a kind of joke, like the funny little trolley in the newspaper comics. It's just a little train, you see, not going anywhere important."

"What was that other thing you called it? What's that mean?"

"The Grim Reaper? Well, that's a kind of joke too. You see there's three railway crossings round and about Norwich. There's signs posted and the trains are supposed to slow down and whistle, but most times they don't. People forget to keep a watch out and...well, that little train's killed more folks...about three a year for as long as I can remember. So we call it the Grim Reaper. That's death, you see. A funny word for death."

I thought about this train, death dressed up as a kind of joke, until Grandpa suddenly turned left and slackened the reins. The horses trotted briskly along a lane shaded by lombardy poplars towards a huge sprawling house with white porches and gingerbread decorating the eaves.

We drove around the back and stopped. There was Gramma, running out of the house and holding me against her soft front, which smelt of cooking and freshly ironed clothes. And Aunt Rose, a younger prettier copy of Mom. We were still standing out there when the old Ford chugged steaming into the yard and Dad and Mom climbed out. Mom had a bright spot of pink in each cheek and her hair was neatly pinned up under her hat.

"Lily!" Aunt Rose rushed over to her. "Come in. You must be exhausted." She went on as if Mom was a visitor to her own home. The pink patches on Mom's cheeks grew brighter. But at last everyone stopped talking and went inside for supper.

We ate around an enormous table in the middle of the vast kitchen. There was Grandpa and Gramma, Aunt Rose, Dad and Mom and me and a little old woman, like a prune. As soon as we were sitting I reached out for a piece of bread. I was starving.

"Manners, manners!" A bony finger as hard as an iron bar rapped the back of my hand.

"Ouch!" I pulled back my stinging hand and stared into a pair of snapping black eyes. That had to be Greatgramma. Mom had warned me about her. Huddled in her chair next to the fire she didn't seem to be much bigger than me; she was all bones with brown wrinkled skin over them, at least over her face and hands which was all I ever did see of Greatgramma, because the rest was covered with a dark print dress that buttoned up to her neck, and long sleeves that buttoned down to her wrists. Her skirts came down to the top of her button boots and a little cap covered her wispy white hair.

That's one scary old lady, I thought, and I kept an eye on her all the time I was spooning up my chicken and dumplings. My, Gramma was a great cook. Even sitting opposite Greatgramma couldn't take away my appetite for her food.

I felt Mom's body stiffen beside me and I started to listen in to what was going on.

"It's so nice to have you back home, Lil," Aunt Rose was saying in a very artificial uppity kind of voice. "We're just going to have to cheer you up and help you forget all the sad things that have happened."

She looked sideways at Dad. He paid no attention, but just buttered another piece of bread. Rose went on and on, her voice getting more and more affected. Mom's arm was touching mine, and I could feel it getting hotter and hotter. In another minute she'll blow right up, I thought.

I caught sight of Greatgramma. She looked like a snake, the way she was watching Mom. I saw her tongue, thin like a lizard's, flick out and moisten her wrinkled lips. Her black eyes darted from Mom to Aunt Rose and back, like she was waiting for something to happen.

Then Gramma interrupted in her soft voice. She never raised her voice, not in all the years I knew her.

"That's quite enough, Rose. Lil, dear, will you help me with the hem of my dress after supper? You were always so good at sewing."

Mom smiled. "Of course I will, Ma."

I drew a breath. The storm was over. Then I saw Greatgramma's face. Her mouth was drooping like a child's when a treat has been taken away. Yes, I'm going to have to watch out for *you*, I thought.

So that first week I kept my eyes open and didn't say much, especially when Greatgramma was around. But I managed to explore the house and farm thoroughly. It was so different from home that at first I lived in a daily excitement of finding something new and strange. It was all so large — like Grandpa, somehow larger than life.

My bedroom faced east instead of north, and my bed had a huge pine frame instead of a rickety brass one with knobs you could unscrew. There was a wash stand with a blue and white patterned jug and basin, a pine dressing table with more drawers than I would ever need for my few clothes, and an old chiffonier with curly fronts and a mirror that reflected cloudily the big pink roses in the wallpaper.

Gramma and Grandpa and Aunt Rose and Mom and Dad and the hired man slept upstairs too, and there was still empty bedrooms to spare. And these rooms were full of heavy old-fashioned furniture, instead of emptiness and dust balls like our bedrooms back home.

The stairs were very grand, of dark polished wood, which shone red and blue and yellow when the sun came through the stained glass window that stretched from the landing to the upstairs ceiling. Downstairs was the never-used parlour, the huge farm kitchen, a half-finished bathroom and the bedroom belonging to Greatgramma.

The farm, too, was larger than life and full of surprises. There was an apple orchard and a sugar bush and a big stand of hickories. Way down at the bottom, next to the wood lot, was a piece of land where a big company wanted to drill for oil.

"We'll all be rich!" Aunt Rose's eyes glowed the day the letter came from Toronto. But Grandpa just laughed. He laughed when the men turned up with their trucks and drilling rig. And he laughed when they packed up and left without finding a drop of oil. But when he saw the mound of subsoil they'd left heaped up in the bottom field it was different.

"Why, those swindlers," he said. "Yank the guts out of the earth and leave them hanging." And he went right into town and talked to a lawyer.

"You can't afford to sue a big company like that!" Gramma protested. But I saw the gleam in Grandpa's eye and I understood. Fighting the big oil company was like fighting the soil and the weather. That was what life was supposed to be about. A challenge — not like getting money out of an oil well without lifting a finger to earn it.

Grandpa loved showing off his house. "My kind of place," he beamed. "It's got style. I used to drive by here on my way in to town and I'd say: One day that'll be mine. Then the man who owned it — the county magistrate he was — he up and died and nobody wanted it. Imagine! A fine big place like this."

When Grandpa talked like that Gramma would roll her eyes up comically, and I guessed she was thinking about the fifteen rooms, all of them much larger than necessary, and the furnace that had never worked properly, so the rooms were freezing in winter and we spent all our time by the stove in the huge kitchen that had been built onto the back of the original square house.

After the first excitement of exploring was over I became lonely for my familiar places. The Toonerville

Trolley, chugging between Western Ontario towns, was like a lizard compared with the dragon of the New York Central. Where the NYC had sometimes as many as three sleek black giants to pull the long freight trains, the Toonerville Trolley was small, with a stubby chimney that puffed asthmatically and a cowcatcher in need of a fresh coat of paint. There were seldom more than ten drab green freight cars to count before the faded red caboose.

Mom and Dad were very quiet, not fighting the way they had done at home. Was I missing the fights? Dad was like a ghost, perhaps because Grandpa was such a loud person. And he seemed smaller. Was that because everything in this house was oversized?

Mom was quiet, but smouldering, like a fire that might burst out at any moment. If she and Aunt Rose were friends, making over dresses or trimming hats, Mom was as sweet as sugar and wanting to cuddle me as if I was still a baby. But if Aunt Rose was in a waspish mood or if Greatgramma prodded with her acid tongue, then I learned to stay right out of Mom's way.

The safest place was with Gramma. Back home I'd fed the chickens, but now I was put to collecting the eggs. It was interesting work. The hens would pick the cunningest places to lay them, almost as if they knew I was after them. I got pretty good at reading their minds and outsmarting them. Nothing was as nasty as a boiled egg that had been laid a week or more before and set out in the August sun ever since.

But once I'd found the eggs I had to clean them, and that was horrible. I had to scrape them with a dull knife and scrub off the stains with Bon Ami before drying them and setting them in racks in big wooden crates. By the time I'd cleaned six or seven dozen I couldn't get the smell out of my nostrils.

Twice a week Mr. Goldberg drove in from Brantford to pick up the full crates. Ten cents a dozen he paid, and that cash had to do for anything that might come up, from a new share for the plough to replacing the pan whose bottom had burnt through when the stove got too hot.

"I'm saving for a vacuum cleaner," Gramma confided the first week I was there. "I've put by every cent I could for two years, but it seems that as soon as I get close to what the man wants something else comes up."

The very next week the Electrolux man came by. He was tall, with neat dark hair and a suit that hung from his thin shoulders as if it were still on its hanger. I could see it was only held together by careful darning.

"Come in and sit down, Mr. Fowler." Gramma welcomed him as if he were the king. "This is my grandson, Blaine. Blaine, say how-d'you-do to Mr. Fowler."

After we'd shaken hands I went on with my job of cleaning eggs at the sink. Gramma reached up and brought down the lustreware jug from the high mantelshelf and began to count out nickels and dimes and quarters. Then she sighed.

"Maybe next time, Mr. Fowler. But you'll have a glass of milk and a piece of pie before you go, won't you?"

"Gramma, why d'you feed everyone who comes to the door?" I asked, after Mr. Fowler had eaten his pie very slowly, as if he were making every crumb count, and then walked down the lane with his thin jacket flapping in the breeze. "Why, you even feed the no-good ones."

"Who's to judge if they're no good?" Gramma put her hands on her hips and glared at me. Grandpa, I thought, but I knew enough not to say it aloud. Grandpa divided the tramps and hoboes who came to the door asking for work into "goods" and "no-goods," without a second's hesitation. Like the Lord dividing the sheep from the goats, I thought, after Gramma had read that bit out of her fat family bible the first Sunday we were there.

"So long as the cows yield milk," Gramma went on. "And there's a sack of flour left and a pail of lard, and the trees are giving apples and the bushes berries, I'll send no man away hungry." She put her hand on my shoulder as I stood at the sink scraping those hateful eggs. "There's not a mite of difference between the pain in the empty stomach of a good man or a bad 'un."

I kept my eye on the lustre jug all that month. I saw Mr. Goldberg's money go in and I just dared anyone to take out a cent. It was a lucky month, I guess, for when Mr. Fowler came by the first of September, looking even leaner and hungrier than before, Gramma carefully counted out the quarters and dimes and nickels.

"Why, Mr. Fowler," she said, with a lilt in her voice I'd never heard before. "I do believe I'll take one of your vacuum cleaners."

I stopped cleaning eggs and turned to watch the drama. I had expected that Mr. Fowler would smile, maybe even laugh or dance a jig. But he did none of those things. He sat staring at the little pile of silver on the table; then he put his head down and cried.

It was awful. I could feel my ears getting hot with embarrassment. Grown men didn't cry! I turned round and went on scrubbing the eggs till they shone. Gramma didn't seem to be bothered one bit. She went over to the stove and began to make tea. Then she sat down and patted Mr. Fowler's thin shoulder until he'd finished crying.

He sat up and blew his nose. "I'm sorry, Ma'am. It was just...seeing the money like that. I haven't made a sale since I was down here last. There's gas for the car and nothing coming in. Sally...she's my wife...she's expecting..."

Gramma poured tea into the two willow pattern cups that were all that remained unchipped of a service for twelve. She murmured comfortingly, not saying that much, just that it was a matter of hanging on, day by day, of keeping one's chin above water and having faith that the bad times would come to an end in God's good time. Mr. Fowler drank his tea and some colour came back to his cheeks.

When he left the farm with Gramma's egg money safely in his pocket he also had a pie wrapped in sugar sacking, a jar of elderberry wine "for your wife, to keep up her strength" and some baby clothes that Gramma said happened to be lying in a trunk just taking up space and inviting moths.

"I'll stop by next month and make sure your machine's working right," Mr. Fowler promised.

"I'm sure it'll be just fine. But I'll be glad to have you stop by. I want to hear how Mrs. Fowler's coming along. You're always welcome."

"You're always welcome." I must have heard Gramma say that a thousand times as desperate men walked the roads of Western Ontario looking for work during that last month of summer.

"Ma, you're just crazy to let them in," Aunt Rose protested. "They'll steal the teeth out of your mouth if you don't keep it shut, Pa says."

"Rose is right," said Mom, for once agreeing with her sister. "They say if you don't give them a handout they'll sneak right back and burn down your barn."

"Fiddle," said Gramma; and she went on talking to and feeding everyone who came up the lane to the house. Though there wasn't work, at least they got a glass of milk and a piece of pie before they went on their way.

I'd never in my life met anyone like Gramma. She worked like a whirlwind, and yet there was always a calm around her and she always had a moment for a smile and a hug. Her day started before six, stirring up the stove and heating the porridge she made every night, summer and winter, with the oats Grandpa grew. Then there was stew to be got on the stove for midday dinner. My chore was cleaning and cutting up the vegetables. There were pies to bake, both for dinner and supper. Cakes and cookies went in while the oven was heating up for the pies. Last of all the bread went in. Gramma never seemed to stop baking. A huge metal flour bin stood in the summer kitchen and Gramma made twelve loaves at a time. In a day, or two at the most, they'd be gone and she'd be baking again.

Between dinner and supper there were the chickens to look after, the eggs to collect, the vegetable garden to hoe and butter to churn. As summer turned towards fall we were even busier, putting fruit up in sealers, frying pork and setting it in crocks covered with fat down in the cellar. There were the beans to pick and dry, and nuts to husk. And always, day in and day out, there was water to carry and wood to chop and split.

The cellar was wonderful. The shelves gleamed like jewels with peach and apple and berry. The bins were filled with carrots and turnips, and the crocks with preserved pork and with pickles. Down in Gramma's cellar I felt safe. Down there the depression was a long way off.

Between whiles there was wash day, which came round when the weather was right and Gramma figured that everyone could do with a change of clothes. I had to help with that to, shaving the big block of Sunlight into the water boiling in the big copper.

Everything went in: sheets, dresses, overalls, long underwear, socks so stiff with sweat they could stand up by themselves.

After each load had boiled for long enough it was pulled out and dumped in the washing machine, which was filled with water from the stove reservoir and more Sunlight. I hated wash days. My job was to work the machine by pulling a handle that turned the paddle inside. It took both hands and was even harder work than churning butter, harder and hotter, with the smell too of soap and dirty water.

Finally the clothes were rinsed in tubs of cold water outside and squeezed through the wringer. That looked like fun, but Gramma was always scared of me running my hands through the rollers, so she'd never let me work it. The only good thing about wash day was that when everything was pegged up outside we could all sit around the table in the steamy kitchen and drink huge cups of tea and eat wedges of pie.

At last summer was over. The harvest was in. Everything that could be stored in bottle, crock or bin was down in Gramma's cellar.

"Time for school," said Gramma, one supper time.

"Well, he's not going to Norwich Public School in those overalls," said Mom. "They're just not suitable, and he's grown out of them anyway. You've got to give me some money for an outfit."

"There isn't any." Gramma looked guilty. "I'm sorry, Lil. There was the vacuum cleaner."

Mom glared, but I squeezed Gramma's hand. "I don't mind. Do I *have* to go to school?"

"Look at him. He's an absolute ragamuffin."

"Do I have to...?" I asked again, but no one was listening.

"Ma, what *can* we do? Can you fix something up for him?"

"I can try, dear. I'll look through the trunks upstairs."

In one of the many trunks Gramma found a pair of old-fashioned men's trousers and picked them apart and sponged the material and turned it to make a pair of trousers, long and baggy "to allow for growing some." But what were they to do for a shirt? Any useful cotton material had long ago been used up for dresses and shirts; and everyone, including me, agreed that I couldn't go to a town school in a shirt made out of flour sacks.

In the end Gramma found a man's dress shirt with ruffles down the front and at the wrists. She cut it down and took it in, and it fit pretty good, everyone said. After Aunt Rose cut my hair, with a pudding basin on my head as a guide, and I dressed in the new ruffled shirt and the baggy pants, everyone said I looked just sweet. I should have known that meant trouble.

On the first morning cousin John, who was Uncle Bob's eldest, from his farm down the road, stopped by to walk me to school.

"Miss Montgomery's your teacher. You'd better watch out for her. No sassing, mind," he warned me.

"I wouldn't." I was shocked. Miss Wingate never allowed sassing.

We walked along the tree-lined streets of Norwich, scuffing at the leaves.

"She lives over there." John pointed at a neat brick house. "Don't ever let your ball go in her yard, cause you don't get it back if it does. She's a terror. There's the school."

It was large and square and unwelcoming. Like a prison, I thought. I stopped, but John's hand was behind me, pushing me on.

"There. That's where you go."

Don't leave me, I wanted to cry. But I didn't know

my cousin John well then. He was four years older than me, which was almost grown up. So I said nothing and he left and I was alone.

I stumped in my clumsy farm boots into the classroom. Miss Montgomery looked up and frowned. Later on I was to understand that the frown was as much a part of her as her stiff back and high-necked shirts and long skirts, but at that first moment I thought it was specially for me.

"Come here, you." She crooked a bony finger. "Who are you?"

I walked up to her desk.

"Blaine Williams, ma'am," I managed to say. She looked at me scathingly, from homemade haircut to frilly shirt, baggy pants and worn boots. Then she sniffed and pointed silently to a desk in the third row.

It was a dreadful day, though I blessed Miss Wingate who had taught us well, as I was put to studying Junior Second. I noticed that those who didn't know their answers fared less well. Miss Montgomery kept a long piece of machine belting hanging from a nail right beside the blackboard. Six good whacks to the boy who didn't know his work or whose attention wandered. I concentrated on my work till I was sweating.

The hours crept by, but at last the bell rang for recess. There was no green meadow, like Cornell, but a yard beaten hard by feet till nothing would grow there but pigweed and dandelions. I stood close to the door, wondering who was going to organize the games, when I felt something behind me. I whipped round. Ten or twelve Junior and Senior Second boys were standing looking at me. They edged closer and I smiled nervously. They grinned humourlessly back.

"Yah, yah, fancy pants!"

"D'you wear that pretty shirt to clean out the barn?"

"Sure he does. I can smell him from over here."

"Poo-whee! Move around so the wind's blowing the other way, will ya?"

As they talked, my tormentors moved in on me. "Let me alone," I croaked feebly. Nothing had prepared me for this. I looked wildly around for a teacher, but they were nowhere to be seen. I was to learn later that they always retired for a cup of tea, and nothing short of mayhem would bring them out.

I got a punch from one side and then from the other. Then, mercifully, the bell rang and recess was over. But at lunchtime they were waiting for me. My lunchpail was torn out of my hand and my egg sandwiches spilled in the dirt and ground in. I got mad and ran straight at the closest boy.

"Fancy pants wants to fight, eh?" His name was Bill Blount. His ears stuck out and he had freckles all over his lardy face. He grinned wickedly. "Come on then."

I got in two kicks and a feeble poke before a fist landed square on my nose. I saw stars and sat up slowly to find myself alone with blood pouring from my nose onto my new shirt. When I staggered into class Miss Montgomery looked at me over her wire-framed spectacles.

"We do not permit fighting in *this* school, boy."

"But..." I began to protest. I felt a kind of quiver in the air behind me, and I realized that life would not be worth living if I told the truth. "I'm sorry, Miss Montgomery."

The afternoon seemed to last forever. At the final bell I ran out of the door and bolted down the road for home.

"Yah, yah, fancy pants. Run home to crazy Grandpa!"

That did it. I stopped and turned, my hands doubled into fists.

"He is *not*."

"Want another poke?" Bill Blount pushed past the others. He had a tooth missing, right in front, that made him look like a wild tom cat.

My nose throbbed. I felt I just couldn't bear for it to be hit again. I swallowed a sob and turned and ran.

"Don't tell Grandpa," I begged, as Gramma washed the blood stains from my shirt and ironed it dry for the next day.

"I expect it's just because it's the first day," Gramma comforted me.

But it wasn't. On Wednesday I got a black eye and a cut above the cheekbone, but not until after school, so Miss Montgomery didn't ask any questions. At supper everyone stared interestedly at my swollen face.

"I hope you won, boy," said Grandpa.

I went on eating supper carefully. I'd just discovered that one of my teeth was loose.

Night after night I lay curled up in bed, longing for the familiar sound of the big trains and the comforting wind in the mulberry tree, and wept into my pillow. By Friday things were no better and I'd made up my mind.

"I'm not going back to school."

"Nonsense. Of course you are."

"I won't and you can't make me." I faced the circle of familiar faces at the supper table as desperately as if it were the circle of my tormentors. "I won't wear those clothes again. The others beat up on me every day. I won't go."

"You've got to learn to fight back," said Grandpa, as I had known he would. "Don't stand for their malarky."

"But they're bigger than he is, Alistair," Gramma argued. Aunt Rose chimed in, and Greatgramma watched with a gleam in her dried-currant eyes.

Dad said nothing at all. When everyone had talked themselves out he pushed back his chair.

"I'll take you into Norwich tomorrow for a couple

of decent shirts and a pair of pants. D'you think you could handle it then?"

I nodded, speechless with gratitude.

"And what'll you use for money?" Mom snapped.

Dad flushed. I held my breath waiting for his answer. I knew Mom and Dad were working for their keep, nothing more.

"Never you mind, Lil," was all Dad said, and first thing Saturday he took the buggy into Norwich with me sitting beside him.

It was almost like old times. I leaned against his arm and he looked down at me and half smiled. When we got to the main street Dad jumped down and handed me the reins.

"I'll be back in a moment," he said and strode off.

When he got back he hitched Pie's reins to a post and took me into the dry goods store to pick out shirts and pants.

"You'd be wise to pick a size larger, so he can grow into them," the clerk suggested.

Dad shook his head. "Nope. He's going to look good right now. Not a year from now when the shirts are wore out anyways." He smacked the coins down on the counter and we walked out triumphantly.

As we drove home I listened to the jingle of change in Dad's pocket. He hadn't jingled on the way into town. A terrible thought crept into my mind.

"Oh, Dad, you didn't rob a bank, did you?"

He turned and stared and then he threw his head back and laughed, the way he hadn't done in months.

"Nope," he said, when he'd done laughing and wiped his eyes. "You can wear those shirts with a clear conscience. I wish I could do more for you."

"Oh, *Dad*."

As we drove along the road to the farm he began to whistle 'Redwing.'

It wasn't until Sunday breakfast that I noticed Dad's watch was gone. It was a pocket chronometer with a chain so it couldn't get lost. But it *had*.

"I'll help you look for it, Dad. I'm great at finding things."

"It's all right, son." His cheeks were suddenly flushed.

"But I'd like to, honest."

"Don't know where it went exactly. Don't worry about it, son."

"I know." Everyone looked up at Greatgramma's cracked voice. She smirked. "You had it on when you went into Norwich yesterday, and you didn't have it when you got back."

Everyone stared at Dad. He looked at the tablecloth and said nothing. Mom stood up, flushed all the way from her forehead down to her neck.

"You *sold* it, Ed!"

"Be quiet, Lil."

"Don't you tell me to...I have some needs too, you know. You never thought of asking if there was anything I needed, did you?"

Dad pushed his chair away from the table and went out, leaving his breakfast half eaten.

"I'm ashamed of you, Lil Williams," Gramma said softly. That was all — but the way she said it!

I found out later that Dad had not only sold his watch, the only thing of any value he had in the world, but he'd gone over to Uncle Bob's and talked to cousin John.

I went to school on Monday in my new pants and my store-bought shirt, my head high. Today none of the girls giggled. I whizzed through arithmetic faster than anyone else and got it all right. But at recess the same ten boys began to close in on me. If they tear my shirt I'll...I'll kill them, I thought.

They drew back suddenly and I looked around. It was John.

"Hi, Blaine, how's it going?"

"Okay, I guess," I said cautiously. In town school the older boys never talked to the younger ones, the way they had down at Cornell.

"That's good." John nodded and looked at the boys surrounding me. "You ever need me, just holler."

That's all he said, but it sure made a difference. They let me alone after that, and I began to make friends with the quieter boys, the ones who'd been afraid to say hello to me when the bullies were around.

Winter came. It was tough for many people, but Gramma's cellar was well stocked, though by February things were getting tight. There were seven mouths to feed, not including the hired man. We ate potatoes fried in pork fat for breakfast and mashed with gravy and a bit of meat for dinner and supper. On Sundays there was no midday meal, since the only chores were milking the cows and looking after the chickens. So on Sundays breakfast had to last right through till supper.

I had shot up during the last year and I was hungry all the time. Sometimes when the others weren't looking Gramma would slip me a thick slice of bread and sugar just to hold me till suppertime.

When the potatoes ran out there were still beans, and when the beans ran out Grandpa went to town and did some complicated swop with a storekeeper. He came home with several great sacks of rice which, I guess, nobody else wanted. So for the next month we ate fried pork and boiled rice three times a day. I got so I didn't want to look at another dish of boiled rice.

But spring came at last. Everyone got the feeling that, well, we'd survived another winter, and surely *this* year things would start to ease up. The birds sang and the earth smelt sweet. This year Dad'll manage to pay the back taxes on the farm and Mom'll be happy again, I told myself, as I walked along the edge of the road to school with the wild flowers springing up around my boots.

But Mom didn't wait around for any miracle.

"I'm going to Toronto to find work," she said one evening, right in the middle of supper. "I can't stand it here another minute."

Her eyes were shining with a kind of scared defiant look in them and she had a bright spot of colour in each cheek. *Don't go*, I wanted to say. Then I thought: *It's okay. Dad won't let her go. He'll make her stay.*

But Dad didn't say a word. He just kept on spooning up rice and fried pork. He looked thinner than ever. I felt as if a hand was over my heart, squeezing and squeezing till I had no breath left. *Say something*, I willed him.

"Damn foolishness," said Grandpa. "What makes you think *you* could find any work in Toronto?"

"Flighty!" Greatgramma pounded her cane on the floor. "Always was. She'll come to no good in Toronto."

"Lil, my dear, you know perfectly well that your place is here with your husband and son." Gramma's voice was as soft as ever, but her eyes were stern.

Mom looked back and it was like stone grating against stone.

"I've made up my mind, Ma," she said. "I can't stand another year here. I've nothing to call my own. I have to beg for a quarter to make over a dress, just like I was still a kid. I warned Ed it wouldn't work."

"Flighty, flighty!" Greatgramma's cane pounded the floor.

"Mom, *please*." My whisper was lost in the babble.

"She's your wife, Ed. Be a man. Put your foot down." Grandpa's neck reddened as his temper rose.

Dad pushed his chair back and got up.

"Lil'll make up her own mind. She knows what's right and what's wrong. I'm saying nothing."

As far as I know he never did, not even when they were alone in the bedroom down the hall from mine. Next day Mom packed a small shabby suitcase and walked down the lane to catch the bus to Toronto.

"I'll walk the whole way if I have to," she had threatened, and Gramma had given her some egg money.

I watched her go, with my heart saying: *Mom, don't leave me. I love you. I can't live without you. You're part of my life.* But my throat was dry and I said nothing.

"Goodbye, Blaine." She hugged me. "You're like me. Dreams are important to you. One day you'll understand why I've got to go. One day you'll take the train and get out of here."

She pushed me away and turned, her mouth a funny square shape, as if she were trying not to cry. She didn't wave when she got to the milkstand by the road, though I was waiting on the porch for her to turn. A car went by and then stopped. She ran after it, jumped in and was gone.

By next Saturday, when Gramma had to go into Norwich, every person we met knew that Mrs. Williams had gone off and left her husband and son.

"What a shame," said Mrs. Richardson at the Post Office. "Poor little boy."

"We all have to make sacrifices these days." Gramma clutched her old black bag fiercely. "Once she's settled in she'll be sending money home. My son-in-law is planning right now to buy a farm as soon as things pick up."

A great weight fell off my shoulders at her words. When we got back I could hardly wait to talk to Dad. A new farm!

"What the dickens is the boy on about?" Dad asked.

Gramma blushed. I looked from one to another, not understanding.

"All I did was explain to Mrs. Richardson how Lil would save money," she said. "Towards a place of your own. One day. She's a good girl, Ed."

"Yes, Ma." Dad went back to seeding without finishing his dinner. Slowly I began to realize that there wasn't going to be a new farm, not ever.

FIVE

Naturally the guys in school got to hear about Mom. They never dared say anything while John was around, but they managed, in many small ways, to make life miserable; I was thankful when school was over and I was able to stay home and help with the haying. This was the second haying this year, and the barn was filled almost to the roof. The weather held steady and only the ordinary number of things went wrong.

Then, between haying and getting in the wheat, the Toonerville Trolley nearly lived up to its other name of the Grim Reaper. Grandpa had taken a full load of tomatoes to the canning factory, driving the old truck that he'd made out of a Model T. Gramma and I were in the kitchen when Mrs. Amery came running in, all out of breath, to say that Grandpa and the train had met at the second crossing.

"And the cowcatcher snagged his truck and dragged it clean along the line. Honest to God, Mrs. Cameron, you've never seen such a sight. Squashed tomatoes along half a mile of line. Mercy, at first we thought it was your man, or what was left of the poor soul."

Gramma turned chalk white and reached out blindly towards a chair back.

"Grandpa? How's Grandpa?" I yelled, thinking the stupid woman was never going to tell us.

"Oh, we found him sitting in what's left of the cab. They've taken him in to Woodstock. So I said to Mr.

Amery, I said, the least I can do is to drive over to poor Mrs. Cameron with the news and maybe offer her a ride into Woodstock. You wouldn't want to have to wait for the bus. Or is your son-in-law here to help?"

Gramma was gripping the chair back and staring blindly at the old calendar on the kitchen wall, and I don't think she heard a word of Mrs. Amery's chatter.

"Dad's in Tillsonburg for a part for the hay mower," I said. "And Aunt Rose has taken Greatgramma over visiting to Uncle Bob's."

"Well then, Mrs. Cameron, will you come into Woodstock now or wait for them?"

"Gramma!" I shook her arm.

She blinked. "I'll come with you, thank you kindly, Mrs. Amery. I'll just get my purse." She groped for it on the high mantel behind the stove as if she couldn't see it, though it was in plain sight just where she always kept it. I lifted it down for her, wrapped her cold hands around it and said firmly, "I'm coming too." The frozen look on her face scared me, and I didn't want to let her out of my sight.

"Maybe you could leave a bit of a note for the others?" Mrs. Amery suggested, so with a stub of pencil I wrote in my best lettering: *Grandpa hurt. Gone to Woodstock with Mrs. Amery. Love, Gramma and Blaine.* I left it propped against the sugar bowl in the middle of the table.

Mrs. Amery talked every blessed moment of the bumpy drive into Woodstock, while Gramma sat silently, her icy hand clutching mine. She never let go of me until we were in the ward. Then she gave a choking gasp and rushed over to one of the beds. I really don't know how she could tell it was Grandpa. He was wrapped in bandages like the pictures of those Egyptian mummies. Only when I got real close to him could I see the bright blue eyes twinkling out of the bandages.

"Oh, Alistair, you old fool, what have you done to yourself now?"

"Sorry, Maggie. That damn fool train came out of nowhere like a pig without the whistle. Wasted a whole load of tomatoes too."

Gramma gave a most unladylike snort, half laugh, half sob. She wiped her eyes.

"Nothing but catsup now, they tell me. Such carelessness. You should sue the railroad, Alistair. They never do signal the way they're supposed to."

"Forget it, Maggie. It'd just make some lawyer rich." When Grandpa said that I knew he must be hurting bad. He, who always fought. "Apart from the load of tomatoes, there's no harm done," he went on.

"No harm?" Gramma stared down at Grandpa, mummified from top to toe. "No *harm*?" She snorted and walked away. It was about the only time I ever saw her at a loss for words.

But Grandpa was right. Uncle Bob hauled the wreck of the Model T to the Norwich garage, and the bumper was welded back on and the panels hammered flat so the doors would shut. Then he and Dad built a new cab and gave it all a lick of fresh paint and it looked almost as good as it had before. Pulled to the right a bit, though, Grandpa said.

As for Grandpa, they let him out of the hospital as soon as most of the bandages were off. He came home with his face a network of scars, but by the next year you couldn't tell them from the ones that were there before, from the time he'd skidded off the bridge into the river, and the time the threshing machine belt had caught him and thrown him right across the barn onto his head.

"He's real tough, isn't he, Gramma?"

"Yes, Blaine, he's tough all right."

The one good thing that happened as a result of Grandpa's tangle with the Toonerville Trolley was that Charlie Thompson came over to stay and help with the work. He was a real nice man and he used to whittle trains and trucks for me in his spare time.

I found out, from a word here and there, that Charlie and Aunt Rose had been going together for years. But he was the younger son of a neighbour farmer and had no land of his own, so he had to work in the broom factory in town. Whether because of this, or for some inscrutable reason of his own, Grandpa had made up his mind that Charlie Thompson was no damn good.

When Grandpa was in hospital and Charlie around our place all the time, Aunt Rose turned into a new person. She was up before Gramma, getting the stove going, helping with the baking, washing and ironing her dresses; and her temper, which was normally as uncertain as Mom's, was as sweet as sugar.

"Too bad my son ain't here to see the change in Rose," Greatgramma remarked at dinner one midday. "She's that sweet and busy, it's downright amazing. Why, he might even change his mind about letting you have her, eh Mr. Thompson?"

Rose turned bright red and choked on her milk, but Charlie didn't seem one bit bothered.

"I sure hope he will, Mrs. Cameron," he said and went on eating his pie.

Greatgramma's lip stuck out like a spoiled baby's. I kept my elbows in and my eyes on my plate. If Greatgramma was disappointed she'd be looking for a fight somewhere else, and I didn't want it to be with me. She still scared me to death. But my admiration for Charlie went up another notch.

Grandpa came home before harvest, but with a warning from the hospital doctor: "You're not to lift as much as a finger, mind that, Mr. Cameron."

So Dad and Charlie and Uncle Bob and the hired man got the harvest in, helped by the neighbours who were going to rent Grandpa's threshing machine once we were through with it. There was plenty to do, getting dinner for twenty or so people; but it was never a panic, as it had been down on the Cornell farm. There were always enough willing hands and times for gossip and laughter.

Grandpa was in fine humour the day the last of his wheat was threshed and safely in the granary. The weather had held steady and none of the machinery had broken down. He looked around the table loaded with good food.

"Thanks to all of you for your help. Now who'll be having the threshing machine next?"

As soon as that was settled he looked down the table to where Charlie was sitting, his red hair standing out from the others.

"And I guess we won't be needing your help any more, Mr. Thompson, thank you kindly."

In the awful silence that followed this Charlie just nodded quietly. He left the table after thanking Gramma for her cooking. In five minutes he was down with his bag.

"Goodbye, all," he said and walked out the door.

"Dad, how *could* you?" Aunt Rose turned so fast she knocked over a chair. She ran down the lane after Charlie, just as she was, in her crumpled print dress and her stained flour sack apron, her hair all mussed up from the day's work.

The men sat frozen at the table, their eyes politely on their plates. Only I ran over to the porch and saw

Rose catch up with Charlie down by the milk table. I could see them talking and talking, Rose waving her arms about in the way she always did when she got excited. Then they put their arms around each other and started getting lovey-dovey, so I stopped looking.

Greatgramma was rocking to and fro, her black eyes gleaming. Oh, how she loved a ruckus!

"I'll thank you for my dinner if you're all through," she said, when it was obvious that no one was going to move or say anything. "*If* you men have quite finished."

The men shuffled thankfully out and hitched up their wagons, and Gramma served dinner for Greatgramma and me. She hardly ate a bite herself, I noticed, though she must have been starving, with no time for anything since a breakfast snatched at five. Rose didn't come in for her dinner. She's sulking, I thought, and I began to feel mad at her when she didn't come in to help with the dishes, so that I got stuck with all the drying.

The rest of that afternoon and all evening Gramma walked down to the road and back. When it got dark and Rose *still* hadn't come home she went to the phone and asked the operator for the number of Charlie's landlady in Norwich.

"You'll be sorry," Grandpa warned her. "It'll be all over town by morning."

Gramma just twitched her shoulders and didn't answer. We all listened while she talked to Mrs. Patterson, trying to make sense out of only half the conversation. Then she put the phone down and sat heavily at the table.

"Oh, my. Charlie's gone! Said he had a week's holiday coming."

"What about Aunt Rose?" I asked. Living in Grandpa's house was always interesting. "Did she take a holiday too?"

Gramma gave a great sob.

"How could I ask Mrs. Patterson that? But I know. She's gone off with him." She blew her nose and turned on Grandpa. "See what you've done, you proud old fool? Now we've lost Rose too."

Grandpa looked discomfitted, but he bluffed it out. "Never could stand a man with red hair," was all he said, then and later.

For a whole week Gramma wouldn't talk to Grandpa.

"You can tell your Grandpa that dinner's on the table," she'd say to me, though Grandpa was standing right there in the same kitchen.

Grandpa seemed to find it funny.

"Blaine, tell your Gramma that was a mighty nice piece of pie and I wouldn't say no to seconds." Things like that.

I'd start to repeat the message to Gramma, sitting all of eight feet away, and she'd sigh and say, "Oh, never mind, Blaine." Then she'd cut a second slice of pie and pass it along. A couple of times I caught her biting her lip, and I figured she was trying not to laugh and mad at herself for it.

The silence only lasted for a week because Rose and Charlie suddenly arrived in the middle of supper, having got a ride out from the bus depot. I hardly recognized Rose. She was wearing a brand new dress and she'd had her hair cut. She looked kind of happy too. They explained, interrupting each other and laughing, that they'd gone straight to Woodstock to get married and then to Niagara Falls for a honeymoon.

"And I can take Rose back to Mrs. Patterson's and go on working at the broom factory." Charlie suddenly got serious and looked Grandpa straight in the eye. "But Rose has a hankering to stay here. As for me, I sure prefer farming to the factory. So if you've got the mind to let me go on working here for a bit of money I can put by for a farm of my own once this young un's grown and taken over, I'd appreciate it." He nodded towards me and I stared, my mind in a whirl. What did Charlie mean? Would Grandpa's farm be *mine* one day?

"It's up to you, Mr. Cameron," Charlie went on firmly. "Either way. Just say your say and have done."

Grandpa opened his mouth, but before he could say a word about red-haired men not being trustworthy Gramma jumped to her feet.

"We'd love to have you, my dears. We'll turn out the big front room upstairs. Why, it's so warm this evening we can put out the sheets and blankets to air for an hour or two."

Greatgramma rocked and chuckled, waiting for the inevitable explosion. So did I. Grandpa stared up at Gramma. With all the scars cross-hatching his face it was pretty hard to tell what he was thinking. There was a long silence. Then Grandpa dropped his eyes.

"Go ahead, woman. Air the bed if you've a mind to."

That's all that was ever said. Rose and Charlie moved into the big front room and life went on much as it had before. I noticed, though, that in his quiet way Charlie was taking a lot of the weight off Grandpa's shoulders, though he was always careful to make it clear that Grandpa was in charge. "They're advertising a new kind of seed over in Tillsonburg. What do you think, Mr. Cameron?" Things like that, until one day Grandpa said, "Oh, for God's sake stop calling me Mr. Cameron. Call me Pa."

Grandpa was still sitting by the stove, stiff and sore, or out in the yard in a chair, when Mr. and Mrs. McEwan, two old friends of Grandpa and Gramma, came for a visit.

"Heard you'd had a run-in with the Toonerville Trolley," Mr. McEwan said when they arrived. "So we thought we'd drive by and see who won."

They stayed for a week, spinning yarns with Gramma and Grandpa about the long-ago times when they were all young, remembering how they'd ride to barn dances and come home three parts asleep just as the sun was rising, the horses finding their own way back to the stables. I looked at those four wrinkled old people and I simply couldn't imagine it; except now and then Gramma's voice would get a lilt in it and she'd laugh and hold her head in a certain way, and then, just for a second...

After a week Mr. McEwan said, "Well, it's been grand visiting you folks. We'll be off to Toronto in the morning to visit with Mrs. McEwan's widowed sister. I want to look in on the cattle judging at the Ex. What d'you say I take the boy along, just for a couple of days?"

In the seconds between his question and Grandpa's answer my mind raced. *Me* go to the Ex? The Ex! It was a dream I'd never imagined could come true. Sure, I had a ticket. They'd been handed out in school.

The President and Directors of the Canadian National Exhibition request the pleasure of the company of... Miss Montgomery had filled in "Blaine Williams of Norwich Public School"... *at Exhibition City, Toronto, on any day from August 24th to September 8th, 1934.*

But what was the good of a ticket? An oblong of pasteboard couldn't transport me like a magic carpet the hundred miles or so to the gates of the Ex. Until now. I held my breath and prayed that Grandpa wouldn't say no right off, the way he usually did to a favour. Maybe the accident and losing his battle over Aunt Rose and Charlie had softened him up a bit. He hesitated.

"Oh, Grandpa, *please*," I got in before he could say anything.

"You'll have to ask your Dad."

"Can I go, Dad? Can I?"

He rubbed his hand across his chin and looked at me with his gentle grey eyes. "Well, I don't know, Blaine. There'll have to be money for rides and lunches and..."

"Frivolity!" snapped Greatgramma. "Waste of money!"

"I don't care," I gasped. "Dad, I can just *look*."

He smiled, and I knew it was all right."

Then Charlie fished in his pocket and came up with a whole quarter, and Gramma gave me one from the lustreware jug. Then, before bedtime Uncle Bob and John dropped by and John slipped me a dime from the money he'd made that summer picking strawberries. I was rich.

"I wish you could come too, John," I said as I thanked him.

"I'd sooner go on working. I'm saving my money."

"What for?"

"Airplane rides. But don't tell."

Airplanes! I'd have liked to have had a chance to hear more about this, but it had to wait. I went off to bed, practically a millionaire, and lay in my hot room, unable to sleep.

It wasn't just the excitement of going to the Ex, but the realization that Mom was in Toronto. As I lay awake I planned how I was going to find her. There hadn't been a single letter home, but I knew exactly what to do. I'd go to the Toronto Post Office and ask for the address of Lily Williams, who'd come up from Norwich. They'd be able to tell me. After all, Mrs. Richardson, at *our* Post Office, knew about everybody living in Norwich and for miles around. Once I'd got this settled in my mind I was able to go to sleep.

We were up soon after sunrise and set off with a

lunch wrapped in a sugar sack, a bottle of milk, and three jars of Gramma's best jelly for Mrs. McEwan's sister. I had a clean shirt and socks, and my sixty cents in a leather change purse tucked safely in the pocket of my overalls.

The car was a bright blue Chevy, and Mrs. McEwan sat beside Mr. McEwan in the front, while I was tucked in the rumble seat with the suitcases. The dust billowed up around me and I had to keep my mouth shut.

"Hang on real tight and don't get scared," Mr. McEwan warned me. "We'll be hitting close to fifty once we get to the highway."

We bumped into Brantford and onto the King's Highway. Mr. McEwan stepped on the gas. It was scary all right seeing the ditches whizz by on either side. We shot past the outskirts of Hamilton and then had to slow down for all the towns strung along the lake like beads on a string: Burlington, Bronte, Oakville, Port Credit, New Toronto, Mimico.

Oh, this was seeing the world! But as we approached the outskirts of Toronto I began to feel uneasy. It was much, much bigger than I had expected. Would I be able to find Mom, even with the help of the Post Office?

Mr. McEwan drove slowly along, holding the steering wheel very tightly and watching street signs. We passed the Ex, with its banners and balloons, and my heart thumped with anticipation. We chugged on down the street and turned north on Strachan Avenue. A right turn. Then a left. There at last was a brick-faced house with lace curtains in the front room and a plant in a big brass pot.

The old lady who opened the door looked exactly like Mrs. McEwan. She had the same round face, the same pink cheeks, the same dark little eyes behind wire-framed spectacles, and the same white hair in a hard knob on top of her head.

While I hauled the cases out of the back they kissed and told each other how young they were looking. I bent down over the bags to hide my grin. Then we went in. It was a real high-class house, with everything waxed and starched and lace mats everywhere. There was a real bathroom upstairs with a tub that had curly feet like a lion's and brass taps with hot and cold water. When you used the lavatory you had to remember to pull this chain thing. I went twice, it was so interesting.

Mrs. McEwan's sister, Mrs. Potter, made us all sit down to dinner, though we told her that we'd had egg sandwiches not an hour before.

"I'm sure the boy will manage," she said, and piled my plate with cold roast beef and potato salad.

The old ladies talked and talked. The room was hot and airless and I could feel myself getting sleepier and sleepier. My head dropped. Then Mr. McEwan dug me in the ribs and tilted his head towards the door. We crept quietly out.

"They'll be at it for hours yet. Let's take a look in at the Ex, eh, boy?"

We walked down the road and across two sets of railway tracks, and there was the CNE, beyond a huge grey arch with statues and banners, grander even than the war memorial in Norwich.

I handed over my precious ticket and Mr. McEwan got a programme. "That's the Automotive Building on your left," he pointed out. "The History of Transportation. Or what about this? Motion Pictures in the Making?"

I nodded and stared and stumbled along beside him, trying to look in every direction at once. Right ahead was the Midway, and the boulevard curved to the right, with even more huge buildings beside it. And there were people everywhere. Thousands and thousands of people.

Mr. McEwan laughed at my dazed expression. "Tell you what, boy. Today we'll look at the exhibits and stay for the evening show. Then tomorrow I'll look in at the cattle judging and you can go on the Midway."

"But I've only a ticket for one day, sir."

"Don't worry about that, son. Now let's see how much we can look at before it gets dark. Then we'll get our seats in the stands in good time for the show."

Well, that old man just about raced me off my feet. We went through the Automotive Building and the Engineering and Electrical Building, which was full of dozens of modern inventions. Then there was the Manufacturers' Building and the Food Products Building, where there were big line-ups for all sorts of free samples. Mr. McEwan wouldn't waste time standing in line, so I had to rush after him, though I was getting pretty hungry by this time. We went through the Horticultural Building and agreed to leave all that high-class stuff in the Art Gallery and the Music Building, and by then it was time for the show.

I collapsed into my seat in the grandstand with a groan. My feet were throbbing and I longed to take my boots off, but I didn't dare. Suppose I lost them or couldn't get them on again? They were getting pretty small anyway, the way my feet were growing. A man went by with a tray of hot dogs and my mouth watered, but I kept a tight hand on the change purse in my overalls. There was still tomorrow and I'd need my money then.

Then Mr. McEwan winked and dragged out of his pocket a couple of thick beef sandwiches wrapped in one of Mrs. Potter's table napkins. "Thought you might be hungry. I made them up while you were dozing away there.''

By now the stands were packed. Though it was still light the shadows ran right across the platform, so the lights showed up real good. The show began with clowns and elephants and trapeze acts. I yelled and held my breath and clapped and so did everyone else. Then, as the shadows deepened, there was community singing until, all of a sudden, the Royal Canadian Dragoons galloped by, each horse in step with the music. They were so much smarter than Pie and Snow, I couldn't believe it.

The main show began with bands and trumpets, and the lights shone on the scenery, which you could tell was supposed to be a forest with three ships anchored off shore. Jacques Cartier came ashore and gave gifts to the Indians. They put up a big cross and read a bit out of the Bible.

The scene changed to Toronto in 1834, with men in funny uniforms and women in long dresses like they wore in the old days. This was followed by Toronto in 1874, with fire engines drawn by horses, and a man riding a funny bicycle with a huge front wheel and a tiny back one.

Last of all there was a lot of loud music and the lights shone onto the back of the stage, and there was Toronto of today, 1934, with all its modern buildings. Everyone cheered and clapped until they were interrupted by an enormous bang. I thought something terrible had happened, but it was all right. It was fireworks, though it was called a Pyrotechnic Display in the programme. They were white and yellow and blue and red, with bangs that shook your chest inside. There was a wonderful smell like…like…the nearest I could think of was the train on the New York Central.

There was a drum roll, and we all stood up for "God Save the King," and I stumbled through the crowd back to Mrs. Potter's house and up to the tiny room under the eaves. I stripped off my shirt and socks and overalls and fell into bed.

The next thing I knew Mr. McEwan was knocking at the door.

"Seven-thirty. And the judging starts at nine sharp. Better jump to it if you want breakfast!"

Mr. McEwan paid my way in. "That's all right," he said when I stammered my thanks. "Likely I'll meet friends at the judging. Can you amuse yourself all day?"

"Yes, *sir*!"

"Then we'll meet up at the fountain at six. Over by the Horticultural Building, remember?"

"Yes, sir."

"You'll be all right then? Good. Keep your hand on your money. Can't trust city folks. They could rob you blind and you wouldn't even notice. Have fun. Don't be scared. Be careful now and don't get lost." With this contradictory advice Mr. McEwan vanished into the crowd that was heading towards the cattle barns. I was alone.

I walked slowly all the way along to the end of the Midway and back. The rides were so much larger and faster and altogether more dangerous looking than the ones at the Norwich fair that I was scared to go on them. I was pushed to and fro; everyone seemed to be moving much faster than I was used to. In a panic I remembered my money and plunged my hand into my overalls pocket. But it was all right. Gramma's change purse was still safe.

The Fun House. The Tunnel of Love. The Roller Coaster. Sideshows with fish men and living skeletons and the fattest woman in the whole world. I turned a corner to find myself face to face with a huge man, dressed in gold pants with a crimson sash, who breathed out fire.

I ran. I was trodden on and pushed aside. I ran until I came to the comparative calm outside the Midway. I longed for Mr. McEwan. Don't get robbed. Don't get lost. Don't be scared. Have fun.

I found myself standing right outside the Food Products Building, so I told myself that I'd planned that all along. I went in and stuffed myself with free samples of shredded wheat, cheese and crackers, pickles and soup, bologna and pork and beans. I felt a bit sick when I was through, but a drink from the water fountain soon settled my stomach.

Full of food and new courage I went back to the Midway and spent a whole five cents on the Fun House. It was very strange. The floors moved up and down and shook from side to side. I had to step through a barrel that rolled me round and round until I could scramble out and climb a flight of joggling stairs. There was a chair at the top and I sat down for a minute to catch my breath. But then the bottom fell out of the chair and I slid breathlessly down a chute and out into the sunshine and the noise, with my nickel spent and not enough time to slow down and enjoy it. That's the big city, I thought. Nothing but rush, rush.

I joined the line-up for the Roller Coaster and recklessly handed over a whole dime. Then I got scared. Suppose the whole thing fell apart? It looked mighty flimsy. But I was trapped in the front car with a bar across my chest so I couldn't get out, and it was too late.

The cars moved forward up the first hill, balanced for an instant on top and swooped down, leaving my stomach at the top. My hands were glued to the front of the car. I shut my eyes and screamed. Up we went and down again towards the tiny people below. It was scary. It was like flying. It was wonderful.

Then it was over and I staggered out, with a mouth like sand and a throat sore from screaming and bought a glass of orangeade to wash away the dry screams. Then I swaggered off, the equal of everyone at the Ex, and lost five cents in a row trying to win a kewpie doll for Gramma.

When I found the Ferris Wheel I didn't hesitate for a minute, but handed over my money and climbed into one of the brightly painted cars. Slowly the great wheel turned and I was lifted high into the air. I felt like Lindbergh must have, crossing the Atlantic. Now I could understand why John was saving every dime to go flying. Why, I could see clear across Toronto. And how huge it was!

Slowly the wheel sank and rose again. If I spat I reckoned I could hit that man slap on the top of his shiny pink head. But of course I didn't. What would Gramma have said!

Then, quite unexpectedly, I saw her. She was strolling among the bobbing heads and bobbing balloons.

"Mom!"

The car sank slowly and the people on the ground came closer.

"Mom!" I screamed. She'd never hear me above the calliope music, the laughter, the yells.

The wheel stopped, but I was trapped fifteen feet above the ground.

"Mom, wait!" I yelled as loud as I could. Heads turned, but not hers. The wheel jerked and my car sank lower. I didn't take my eyes off her blue polka dot dress. Over by the refreshment stand.

At last it was my turn and I jumped out and pushed past the man unloading the cars. I slammed into a fat man, dodged around him and ran on. The refreshment stand was right in front of me, but she was nowhere in sight. I stared down the main road running through the Midway. I pushed past people lined up in front of the sideshows. I had seen her. I *had*. And I couldn't lose her now.

Out of the Midway crowd I turned this way and that. I ran into buildings and out again, frantically sure that she was just walking by and I'd miss her. By the time I leaned up against the stonework of the fountain, my throat choked with tears, I had run around the grounds at least twice.

"What's the trouble, son? Something scare you?" It was Mr. McEwan. I shook my head and rubbed my sleeve across my face.

"Well, I'm a mite early, but what d'you say? Have you had enough? Are you ready to go back to Mrs. Potter's for a bite?"

I nodded silently. I couldn't have said a word to save my life. As we walked back to the house the panic in my chest began to die down. I'll go to the Post Office tomorrow, I promised myself. They'll tell me where Mom is.

By the time we got to Mrs. Potter's, I was able to talk to the two old ladies about the great day I'd had at the Ex without breaking down and bawling. But I couldn't sleep that night. It was hot under the stiff sheets and the blankets that smelled of mothballs. And the traffic noises never seemed to stop. How could Mom *bear* to live in this crowded stuffy city?

Right after breakfast next day I put my plan into operation.

"Please, may I go for a walk?"

"You won't get lost?"

"No, ma'am."

"This isn't Norwich, you know. You must remember to look both ways…"

Mrs. Potter combed my hair flat and gave me a piece of paper with her address on it and then let me go. At the corner store I asked how to get to the Post Office. It was quite a long walk, but I got lost only once. It was much larger than the Norwich Post Office, but shabby, with notices peeling off the walls. Mrs. Richardson would never have stood for that.

"Please, I'm looking for my Mom's address. Her name's Lily Williams and she's from Norwich." I had rehearsed what I was going to say as I walked along.

The man behind the wicket stared. "There's twelve postal stations and a hundred and fifty substations in Toronto. Why, there's a million people here now, and more on the go with no fixed address. If her name isn't in the phone book I can't help you." He pointed to the phone book and I looked through it. There were pages of Williams', but none was Lily or Mrs. Edward.

"Thank you, sir." I turned to the door. It was a long walk back to Mrs. Potter's.

"Wait a minute, son. There's the police. Have you talked to them? Or get your folks to advertise…you do have folks, don't you, son?"

His voice followed me as I stumbled out. I walked blindly along grey streets. Every time a woman with dark hair walked past I'd turn and look, just in case. My feet throbbed and I got thoroughly lost.

"What's up, son?" He was a wrinkled man with one leg and his cap pulled down over his ears, selling papers. I showed him Mrs. Potter's address.

"Well, you've come a fair way, haven't you? You'd better get a trolley over there. One that'll let you off at Bathurst. Mind you ask now. Bathurst. Got a nickel?"

"Yes, thanks." Luckily I still had a nickel left from

yesterday. The trolley ride would have been exciting if I hadn't felt so wretched. It clattered and rattled noisily across town and let me off a few blocks from Mrs. Potter's.

I was in time for a dinner of mutton stew and treacle pudding. I choked it down while the old folks watched me eat with pleased smiles on their faces. We said goodbye and drove out of Toronto, and I threw up over the side of the car somewhere between Burlington and Hamilton.

SIX

The knowledge, bitter though it was, that I'd better not count on seeing Mom again, helped me grow up. But in my room, watching the sky darken, I thought about her and Dad, wondering what had gone wrong. And I dreamed of escaping myself — one day. I got through Senior Second in Miss Montgomery's classroom, and the following year I went into Miss Turner's room. She wasn't much younger than Miss Montgomery, but she sure was different. For a start, she didn't keep a strap hanging by the blackboard.

I'd been in school a week when she kept me back one afternoon.

"Gee, Miss Turner, what'd I do wrong?"

"Nothing." She laughed. She had a pretty laugh for an old lady. "I'm delighted with your work. Do you have to spend much time doing your homework?"

"I guess not." I had the chores for Gramma and homework, and there was still plenty of time for reading and dreaming.

"What do you like to read?"

"*Treasure Island*. It's the only book I've got. I've read it about a dozen times."

She laughed like an excited kid.

"I'll lend you all the adventure stories you can read, Blaine, if you'll do something for me."

"Sure, Miss Turner. You bet."

"I'd like you to take Junior and Senior Third in one year."

I stared. Was she trying to do herself out of a job?

"Why?"

"Because you're going to get bored. You need the challenge."

She went on to tell me what I'd have to do. Then she said, "Walk me home, Blaine, and I'll let you have a book right now."

She had me wait in her parlour while she ran up to her room. I sat with my elbows tucked in, in mortal fear of knocking over one of the hundred or so china ornaments that cluttered up the room.

"There. *Coral Island*. But don't you dare start it until you've done your homework and your chores. I warn you, it's addictive."

And it sure was hard to put down. After that book there were others, dozens of them. That year was the best time. I worked real hard in school and at home and I started to shoot up. "Like a weed" Gramma said and tried to feed me extra, though things were short near the end of winter.

"Look, Dad, I'm almost as tall as you now."

"So you are, son. That's good." Just for an instant there was a smile on his face. Then it faded and the light went out of his eyes and he was like a grey ghost again.

I felt sad for a while but Uncle Bob and Aunt Mary got in the habit of asking me along on their rare excursions into Tillsonburg or even down to London, and sometimes I got to stay overnight on their farm.

My cousins, Lizbeth and Maggie, were a pain, giggling all the time and acting as if I were about ten years old instead of eleven going on twelve. But John was great. He found the girls as irritating as I did and his little brother Bill was still just a baby. In some ways I think I was like a younger brother he could talk to.

We used to have great times, lying awake after the house was quiet, whispering far into the night, telling each other our secret dreams and fears.

"Last week I got the bus into Tillsonburg and went up in a Tiger Moth. The instructor let me take the controls. He says I'm a natural. I'm going to save up every cent for lessons."

"But what for, John? What'll you do with a licence? You could never afford to buy a plane, could you?" I imagined him barnstorming around the country in a battered biplane.

"Jeez, Blaine, I don't know. But it's something I've got to do. You feel so free up there, like the weight of the depression and all just slides off. Nothing matters any more. Just the sky and the feel of the plane, like you're a part of it. I can't really describe it."

I nodded in the dark. That's the way I felt when I was reading *The Scarlet Pimpernel* and *Anthony Adverse*.

"What about you, Blaine? You'll farm, I suppose."

"I guess I'm going to have to. What else is there but the broom factory? But I want something more. I don't know. Miss Turner says I've got to go to High School, but what's the point?"

Then, in whispers, through one long hot summer night, I shared my dreams about the trains with John. I was scared he might laugh; but it was all I had to share. I described how the trains tore through the night, how they shook the house. "...and Mom always said that if I could count all the cars right, no mistakes, then I'd get my wish."

"Did you count them right?"

"Yes. I think so. Yes, I'm sure I did."

"What'd you wish?"

"To get away from here. To be free."

"Yeah. That's what I'd have wished too." He didn't laugh. We lay in comfortable silence while the memory of my train shook the room. After that night John and I were more than just cousins. Though there were four years between us we were like blood brothers.

In the summer of 1936 I graduated from Senior Third. I'd done it. I'd also read about every one of Miss Turner's books, and I was even crazier to get away from the farm and start living.

I knew it was going to take money. Early in the summer I'd hired myself out to pick strawberries. It was hard work, on my knees evenings and all day Saturday, filling berry boxes at one and a half cents a box. The strawberries tasted real good, but by the end of the season I hadn't made much of a start on my escape money.

"They're still suckering tobacco," John phoned one evening. "I can get you a job down there. It's hard work but it pays three bucks."

"A week?" That didn't seem like much. "And we've only got Saturdays and evenings."

"A day!" John laughed. "Meet me at my place at five."

So the next Saturday I wobbled down the road on Dad's old boneshaker, and John and I biked the five miles down to Van Hoosan's farm. It was on the same sandy soil where Dad had struggled and failed to make a living. Now, with plenty of fertilizers, farmers were finding out it was great for tobacco. If Dad had just hung on and had a bit of luck and a lot of know-how we might have made a fortune. But what's the use of 'if?'

John showed me how to go down the rows of tobacco plants nipping off the new shoots that grew where the leaves joined the stems.

"Just like tomatoes," I said cheerily. It sounded like an easy way to earn money.

"Yup," said Mr. Van Hoosan, and looked at me kind of funny, as if he knew something I didn't.

It was surprisingly cold in the shadows between the rows, where the night air still lingered. The plants were heavy with dew and within five minutes we were soaked to the skin. It was crouching work, worse than strawberries, with the bitter tobacco smell in one's nostrils the whole time and one's hands sticky with tar.

Three dollars a day, I told myself. Three dollars a *day*. At the end of the first long row I stood up to ease my aching back and to warm myself in the sun that was just beginning to shine across the field. I shivered. I was wet and freezing.

"Hey you, young 'un!"

"What's the matter?"

"Get back to work."

That's where I found out the difference between piecework and day labour. With piecework you're pushing yourself to make enough money. With day labour another man's watching and driving you. Three dollars, I told myself, and stooped back to the row.

The sun climbed slowly until it was high enough to dry our shirts. Then it began to bake us, beating down on our heads and shoulders. I hung grimly on, trying to keep level with John. He was four years bigger than me, but my fingers were neater at nipping off the suckers. We came out about even.

By the time the boss yelled "lunchtime" my head was throbbing from the heat, my back ached and my knees were numb. I hobbled back to the beginning of the row where we'd left our lunches and hunkered down next to John to wolf down egg sandwiches in a scrap of shade against a shed. The food was bitter with the tobacco taste and I couldn't get the smell of it out of my nostrils. After a long cold drink from a stand pipe we lay in a bit of shade between the rows to get the kinks out of our backs.

I was just about asleep when 'wham' went the screen door and the boss was yelling "Time. Let's go!" And we crawled down the interminable rows until near sunset.

"You did okay," the boss said to me, and I got three fresh dollar bills to button down carefully in my shirt pocket. We biked the five miles home with hardly a word, weaving from side to side when our tired legs stopped pumping.

Before supper I scrubbed my hands, but I couldn't get the stains off. I looked like a chain smoker. But that was okay. It was the stain of real money, and that was something we hadn't seen much of for as long as I could remember. I gave the three dollars to Gramma to look after.

"And some for my keep. It's only fair."

"We'll see," she said, as she put it safely away in the old green cash box with the family papers and the deed to the farm.

By the time John and I had to stay home to help with the harvest we'd saved the best part of twelve dollars each. It was a fortune.

"I'm proud of you, son," Dad said. "Only...don't forget about the other things..."

"What d'you mean, Dad?"

"Like dreaming and reading. Don't get all eaten up with the idea of money. It's not everything."

"But you need it to..." I stopped. I didn't want Dad to know that I still felt the way Mom did, wanting to escape.

We got a good harvest that year, with the sky clear day

after day and the dew not too heavy. The threshers came in and Aunt Rose and I helped Gramma in the kitchen.

On the final day, after the threshing crew had left, I was helping Gramma put the last of the dishes away. Grandpa and Dad, Charlie and Sam, the hired man, were sitting at the table, too tired to talk or move. Aunt Rose had just got a lift into Norwich to stay over for a friend's wedding in the morning.

Uncle Charlie groaned and stretched. "Well, I'm for my bed." The others made a move and Sam went out to check the stock. Then we heard him yelling.

"What the devil?" Grandpa threw the door open. Sam stumbled into the room, so out of breath he could hardly talk.

"Fire, Mr. Cameron. Out in the barn!"

I was just about to run after the men when Gramma caught my arm.

"Phone the fire department, Blaine. I'm just too shaky to do it."

I pressed the button and cranked the handle like mad until the operator came on the line.

"Fire Department, hurry!" I said importantly. They came on the line at once, so I knew they weren't out on another call. I explained to Mr. Bates. His son Tom was in my class.

"I'm sorry, Blaine. There's nothing I can do."

"What d'you *mean*? Grandpa's barn's burning. What if the house catches? What if..."

"Sorry, Blaine. We've got jurisdiction right out to the north side of the concession road. Your Grandpa's farm's on the wrong side of the road."

Though I begged and pleaded, nothing would make him change his mind. And there *were* no other fire engines but the town ones. I slammed the phone down and ran out. Smoke was oozing between the shingles as well as pouring out of the end window. Charlie had heaved the ladder against the end wall and he and Grandpa and Dad and Sam were passing pails of water along from the pump up the ladder and in through the window.

I could tell it wasn't going to be enough. They might as well have been spitting on it. The smoke got suddenly thicker, and a yellow flame licked across the window sill and singed Charlie's red hair. He ducked quickly, then climbed down and hauled the ladder away so it wouldn't get burned. Then they began to drive out the horses and cows from the bottom of the barn.

The chickens! I thought and ran. But have you ever tried to make a couple of hundred chickens do what you want? As fast as I shooed them out of the barn they scuttled back in. It was time to roost and that was that.

"Stupid birds," I yelled, with tears of anger and irritation from the smoke running down my face. "Don't you know you'll be killed!"

Grandpa and Dad and Uncle Charlie began to drag the equipment out of the lower floor of the barn, with Sam, the hired man, working just as furiously as the others. Now the flames were licking through the roof and sparks were beginning to fly. I helped haul water to wet down the roofs of the outbuildings that lay between the barn and the house. We prayed the wind wouldn't change.

"Blaine! Blaine, come here!" It was Gramma. I ran into the house. "You stay away from the barn, d'you hear me? Find a safe place outside and watch the roof of the house."

"But, Gramma…"

"Do it, Blaine. If it catches I'll need time to get Greatgramma out."

Greatgramma was sitting like a silent shadow, dressed as precisely as ever, but the crooked hands that clutched the handle of her cane were white and her eyes were tight shut. On the table were Gramma's old black purse and the green cash box. The room was dark and I went to pull up the window blind, but Gramma stopped me.

"We don't want to see the flames, Blaine."

"All right, Gramma. Don't worry. I'll look out for you." I ran outside. The flames licked hungrily at the rafters and the support beams. You could see right through the roof now to the sky beyond, which was a strange pink colour, like before a storm. If only it *would* rain, I thought. But it was just the reflection of the fire.

I went around the side of the house, checking the roof. Down at the bottom of the lane there were dozens of cars and buggies parked along the concession road. Hundreds of eyes out there in the darkness watching Grandpa's barn burn down. Like the eyes at the auction.

Go away! Leave us alone if you won't help, I wanted to yell at them. But they couldn't help anyway. The pump had already run dry. I clenched my fists and went around the other side of the house away from the road, and climbed into the front seat of Grandpa's old Buick. From there I could see the barn and outbuildings, and keep an eye on the house roof.

With a crash and a fountain of sparks the rooftree collapsed. As the remains of the rafters fell with it into the smouldering straw below they stirred up fresh air. Flames and sparks shot up with a roar like the roar of the train.

The night darkened and the fire slowly died. I waited and watched until dawn came. I crawled out of the car, shivering, my eyes as scratchy as if I hadn't slept for a week, and walked around the back of the house.

Grandpa was standing by the barn, staring at the charcoaled timbered ends sticking out above the stone foundation.

"There goes a life's work," he said, as calmly as if he were telling a story of long ago. "A year's wheat and oats, and hay and silage for thirty cows and four horses."

"I'm sorry about the chickens, Grandpa."

"You did your best. Fool birds never know what's best for them. Well, at least the fire didn't catch the house. Time for bed, boy. We've a couple of hours before milking."

I kicked off my boots and fell into bed just as I was, and didn't wake until noon. For a moment I stared at the black smears on my pillow and my filthy hands. Then I remembered and ran downstairs.

Dad and Charlie and Sam had already hand-milked all thirty cows, and Grandpa was poking around in the smoking debris. You couldn't get too close. The stone foundation was still almost as hot as an oven on baking day.

"Soon as it's cool we'll cart it away and start over," he said, half to me, half to himself. "Bigger this time. That old barn was never big enough for my liking."

I looked up into his bright blue eyes and hugged him. What a man! I went right back into the house to tell Gramma that we were going to rebuild the barn.

"And will you please put my tobacco money towards it?"

I ran outside again. It was a clear glorious day. Part of me was proud to be part of Grandpa's dream. The other part snarled inside me: *Why did you do that, Stupid? Now you'll never get away.*

Dad left the farm that September. He got a job in

Tillsonburg, not much I reckon, and at the time I couldn't figure out why he'd want to leave me and the comfortable farm.

"I'll drop by to see you," he said. "And there's an old trunk in my room. It's yours."

The trunk was filled with books, many of them ones I'd already borrowed from Miss Turner, others I'd never read. And there were dozens of old copies of *National Geographic*. All the years I'd dreamed of books and read and re-read my *Treasure Island*, Dad had this wonderful collection right in the house. I'll never understand him, I thought, as I settled in to read.

I hardly missed Dad at all. He'd been a shadow for a long time, even before Mom left. School started and I walked along the road, dreading the first day. What would the new teacher be like? Would I still be able to stand up against Bill Blount? Then I thought of Grandpa. He'd already started to rebuild his barn on the stone foundations of the old one. And it was going to be bigger and better. Well, if he could handle the fire like that, I could surely handle school.

I squared my thin shoulders and walked so briskly along the Norwich road I caught up with Susan White, without in the least meaning to.

The White farm was down the road a piece from ours. Susan's brother Arnie was probably ahead of her. I wouldn't mind catching up with him and having his company the first day of school. I sped up to pass Susan, but she turned and looked at me just as I got level. I found myself slowing down, walking beside her, while part of myself was asking: *Blaine, are you crazy? The boys'll really razz you now.* The other part of me was snared by the helplessness in Susan's hazel eyes.

She didn't say anything and neither did I. When we reached the school yard who should be hanging around but Bill and Joe.

"Well, lookee, who's walking little Missy Two-Shoes to school!"

"How d'you suppose she can stand the smell?"

"She's off the farm herself, silly. That's how come she doesn't notice."

Something of Grandpa boiled up in me.

"Walk you home after school," I commanded Susan. She nodded and her cheeks went pink so that she looked almost pretty. When she had run past Bill and Joe I turned to them. "Okay, fellas. Want to make something of it?"

I couldn't believe what happened. Joe backed right off. Bill looked at Joe and back at me and hesitated. *Why*, I thought, *he may be a year older than me, but he's spent the whole summer in his Dad's bakery eating doughnuts. I could take him apart.* Luckily, before I had to prove this thought, the bell rang. I walked right past the two of them into school. My heart was thudding against my ribs, but I felt real good.

After that I walked Susan home from school most days. That is to say, I carried her books as far as the bottom of our lane. Then I handed them over and said "See you tomorrow."

One day I went into the house to find Aunt Rose leaning against the sink killing herself laughing.

"You call that walking your girl home?" she spluttered. "Letting her go the last mile alone?"

I dumped my homework on the kitchen table and stared.

"If I walked her all the way home I'd have to walk the extra mile back here. That's dumb."

Grandpa laughed. "That's the way, boy. Don't let the ladies pull the wool over your eyes."

Though they went on teasing me about my "new girl" the words just rolled off me. Walking with Susan gave me a sort of grown-up feeling, as if she needed protecting. She was the quietest person I ever knew, and I found her kind of restful.

When I wanted a bit more excitement I'd meet up with her brother Arnie and Jock Ferguson, both of whom were in Junior Fourth. Jock's father also farmed a bit south of us. He was a wild Scot who got roaring drunk every Hogmanay, though he never touched a drop the rest of the year.

Whenever Jock and Arnie and I felt like getting up to some mischief, such as walking the school fence, which was strictly forbidden, or stealing apples from people's gardens, Susan would hang around like a small reproachful shadow, her books hugged against her thin chest.

"Go on home, will ya?" Arnie would yell.

"Nah, let her stay," I'd reply, if I was in a generous mood. "She's not in the way. She can act as lookout." Then Susan would colour up and her eyes would get kind of sparkly.

"Geez, Blaine, it's fine and dandy for you. You don't have no kid sisters hanging round all day. Give me a break."

"Okay, Susan, off you go."

Then she'd walk obediently away, with her head down so that her blonde braids fell forward exposing her pale neck. That neck could reproach me as she never did in words.

Darn it, I thought. *Why does she have to make me feel guilty? I don't owe her a thing.*

To push the memory of that small meek neck out of my mind I'd think up something extra hell-raising to do, like stealing the apples right out of Miss Montgomery's yard, which was about as smart as stealing the devil's pitchfork right out of you-know-where.

We got away with it once, but the second time we

weren't so lucky. She must have been peeking right through her lace curtains at us.

"God almighty! What a fuss over a few apples!" Grandpa swore, after Miss Montgomery had complained to the policeman and made him come right out to the farm. She had us whipped too, with her special strap, and threatened to have us suspended from school.

Grandpa, still fuming, packed a crate of his own apples and drove over to Miss Montgomery's with them. She sent him smartly home again. It was the only time I ever saw Grandpa worsted in an argument.

For Christmas that year I got skates, in spite of the fact that money was real tight, what with paying for the new barn and for hay for the stock. At last I could join the other guys on the pond, with my new skates strapped to my boots, whacking a flat stone about with sticks, pretending that we were great hockey players.

Skating was so much fun that I got in the habit of hanging about in town after school. Then I'd be late for my chores and catch heck from both Gramma and Grandpa. I didn't get heck from Susan for not walking her home any more. She just reproached me silently with her big hazel eyes and her white neck, until I got mad and told her flat out not to bother me.

The ice melted and the hockey games were over. The ditches outside town filled with ice water. Jock and Arnie and I raced home, trying to trip each other into the ditch. Gee, that water could sure make you yell, running down inside your collar and flooding your boots.

"You'll catch your death," Gramma scolded, after a real dunking. She began stripping off my clothes right there in the kitchen.

"Hey, quit that, Gramma. I'm not a kid anymore," I yelled, battling for the right to keep on my long johns.

"Then quit behaving like a kid. Oh, go on then. Get upstairs and find something dry to put on."

In the end it was Arnie, not me, who caught cold. He was home for a week and then he was fine, with just a bit of a cough. But Susan caught his cold. Then I heard she'd come down with pneumonia.

"Little girls don't get pneumonia. Only old people," I said when I heard.

Gramma said nothing. She'd lost two of her children back in 1911 and 1912, but that was the *old* days. Surely that didn't happen now?

Aunt Rose echoed my thoughts. "1937. You think by now they'd have a cure."

"She's not really going to *die*, is she?" This was the first time that death had reached out to someone I knew well, not counting Grandpa's brush with the Toonerville Trolley. Could death touch us, the young?

The news came over the phone one evening when I was wrestling with an algebra problem, not even giving a passing thought to her.

Aunt Rose turned from the phone and said, "Why, little Susan White's dead!" Just like that.

I put down my pencil and walked out of the house, past the barn and the hundred-acre field to the sugar bush. The ground was drying out nicely and there was spring beauty and trillium everywhere.

I thought about Susan not being there any more, not this spring, not any spring. I tried to think of her in heaven, with wings and a halo, but she still seemed unhappy. No matter how hard I tried I couldn't imagine her face, only her back view, with her blonde braids falling forward, showing her thin defenceless neck.

Why hadn't I been nicer to her? If only I hadn't told

her to get lost. That was a terrible thing to say to a person. *Get lost*. Now she was. And it was all my fault.

Then I began to get mad. "You didn't have to hang around all the time like that!" I shouted up at the sugar maples. "Guys need to be alone once in a while. And you weren't that special, you know!"

I realized that was true. She *hadn't* been that special. What I'd liked about Susan was the power she gave me, to be kind and protective, or to send her obediently away. She had made me feel important and grown-up.

I hated myself. I put my head down on my knees and bawled. When I'd finished I wiped my face on my sleeve and said aloud, "I'm sorry, Susan. I'll never hurt another girl's feelings like that, I swear. And I won't go out with anyone until I know for sure it's for real." In my mind Susan turned and gave me a small smile. Then she vanished. But that promise got me into trouble lots of times before I got settled.

Facing Arnie was difficult. For a time I could hardly bear to look him in the eye, and I felt stiff and stupid talking to him. Then one day, when we were walking back from school, he said, "Susie always had weak lungs, the doctor said. If it hadn't been the pneumonia it'd have been something else, like TB maybe."

It wasn't much consolation, but at least I didn't feel quite such a murderer for pushing Arnie in the ditch so that he gave Susan his cold. But school was soured for me that year. I couldn't wait for it to be over.

As soon as we were let out I hired on full time at Van Hoosan's. I'd already been suckering every Saturday since June. Now I had to learn to be a handler. It was better pay, but it was still the worst and most mindless job I ever had. We worked at it top speed, from early morning to sunset, rain or shine.

The primers brought in the boxes full of yellow

leaves they'd picked; they were laid on tables and us handlers had to pick up three leaves at a time and hand them to the tier so the stalks were just right. She'd whip the string into a hitch around the leaf stalks on one side of the drying pole, three more in a hitch on the other side, and so on until the pole was full.

A good tier could make twenty-five dollars a day piecework, taking the leaves from two handlers. If you weren't fast enough or held the leaves wrong they'd swear something fierce. By the end of the day we were exhausted, our hands and clothes sticky with tobacco juice, and the leaf tiers' hands and arms swollen from the constant irritation.

After a day at Van Hoosan's John and I would bike silently home. I used to try to wash off the sticky stuff before eating, but the taste was in my mouth and nose. I'd fall into bed and sleep with the smell of it on me, and wake with a start from a dream of handing leaves...one, two, three...one, two, three... Over and over through the night until my alarm clock shook me awake and I'd shiver my way sleepily downstairs to a bowl of Gramma's hot porridge. Then down the road to pick up John at the bottom of his lane, with a honey pail full of sandwiches over the handlebars of my bike.

Once a week I had to go alone, when John went into Tillsonburg for flying lessons. I envied him those days in the clean blue sky, and wondered where and when *my* escape would come.

That August was a blur of mind-numbing work and smouldering anger. I was angry with Susan for dying, at Mom for leaving me, at Dad for being what he was: a failed farmer, a quiet and unforceful man. I was angry at life and the depression, which made the future seem so hopeless.

Then summer was over and I was in Senior Fourth.

John was going into Fourth Form in High School, but he had his pilot's licence and was bent on leaving school.

"Maybe I could join a barnstorming group. I could look after the plane. I don't care."

"It's awfully dangerous, isn't it?" I'd seen them just that summer, a group landing in a field north of town. The pilots had looped the loop, stalled, fallen out of the sky in what looked like uncontrollable spins, only to pull out at the very last minute, just feet off the ground.

"Not if you know what you're doing. It'll get me out of here."

"What about the farm?" John was Uncle Bob's elder son.

"Hang the farm. He can leave it to Bill for all I care. I want to make something of my life right *now*, not wait for thirty years till Dad gets too old and wants me to take over. I want to live *now*."

SEVEN

Once I was back in school and the tobacco harvest was over, time began to drag. It was not that there was nothing to do; with money about — tobacco money — there were parties, dances and picnics. There was a change, too, in the attitude of the townspeople. This new money was from the despised farms, and suddenly it wasn't so bad to be a country boy. Even people like me, from the old mixed farms, where we still had to struggle to make ends meet, noticed the difference.

But I just didn't seem to be a part of it. For one thing I felt more awkward than ever. I'd shot up about four inches that summer, and my voice was unreliable. Some days it'd be fine; but on others it'd suddenly boom or squeak, usually just when I was called on to answer a question in class. Then the boys would guffaw and the girls would giggle.

Charlie caught me one day staring gloomily into the spotted mirror in my room. My hair was limp, my face was thin so that the bones of my jaw and forehead stuck out like a skull. I was thinking about death when he lounged by.

"What's up, Blaine? Missing your Dad?"

"I guess." Guiltily I realized that I hadn't even thought of Dad in days.

"I could drive you down to Tillsonburg Saturday. Visit him."

"No!" I said violently. Trying to talk with Dad in this mood would be torture.

"Oh, leave him alone, Charlie." Rose came up behind him. I could see her hands on his shoulders, in the mirror, kind of loving, and I felt more alone than ever. "It's just his age. He'll grow out of it."

After they'd gone I thought maybe if I'd told Charlie everything that was going on in my head I'd feel better. But I knew that wasn't true. I didn't even understand myself what was happening to me.

It got so that I just couldn't bear to be around people at all. As soon as school was over for the day I'd walk home as fast as I could with the excuse of homework. In fact it would take me no more than an hour; then I'd whip through whatever chores Gramma had set me and hightail across the farm to the sugar bush where I could be alone. Even books were no good any more.

On Saturdays and Sundays I'd take a packed lunch with me and head off along the concession road, either east or west, cutting down lanes and across country, not going anywhere, just mindlessly walking, kicking up the heaps of brilliant leaves, smelling the bitter-sweet death smell of fall, listening to the lonesome cry of geese skeining across the sky and the raucous call of marauding crows. When I came to a little town or even a village I'd skirt around it, so strong was my need to be alone.

Then I met Goldie. That's what I called her anyway. I was way off east somewhere past Kelvin, I guess, when she hobbled out of a ditch, where she'd been lying licking her foot, and began to follow me.

"Go on now," I said after a while. "Go home."

She stood in the middle of the lane with her tongue lolling out and a foolish smile on her face. I didn't know what breed she was, mixed farmyard I supposed at the time, but I could tell there was a lot of golden retriever in her. She looked at me, waving her tail like a plume. I looked back at her and found myself saying, "Well, okay. Come on then if you're coming," and I headed off home without looking over my shoulder.

She didn't hesitate for a minute. She made a rush at my legs. Then she limped ahead, over the rise and out of sight. When I got to the top she was waiting for me, laughing. I threw maybe a couple of sticks for her to retrieve, but I didn't pay that much attention to her; yet she was still close at heel when I opened the kitchen door.

"She's a real beauty, Blaine. But I hope you're not set on keeping her. You know your Grandpa and dogs."

Gramma was right. There wasn't a dog on the place. For as long as I'd known Grandpa there'd never been a dog. But the funny thing was that until Gramma warned me I hadn't seriously thought of keeping Goldie. She was just a dog who'd happened by on a Saturday walk. Suddenly it began to matter.

"Does he hate them that bad? Couldn't I keep her out in the yard. Maybe build a doghouse for her...?"

My words faded as Gramma shook her head.

"Hate dogs? Mercy, no, boy! He always loved them dearly. But he had an old German shepherd once, called him Foxy because of his bushy tail..."

"And?" I prompted.

"Well, one day Foxy and your Grandpa were coming along the concession road over there. Your Grandpa'd just crossed the railway line and Foxy was still on the far side worrying at something he'd found in the ditch. Then a train came along the line. Foxy's ears pricked up and he was out of the ditch and bounding towards your Grandpa. Well, he yelled — lordy, I remember I heard him in the kitchen, he yelled so loud — and I ran out of the house to see what was the matter. 'Keep back, you fool dog. Keep back,' he yelled. But Foxy just heard his voice and ran towards it.''

"So the Toonerville Trolley killed Foxy too?"

"The cowcatcher just picked him up and tossed him aside and kept going. Grandpa yelled at the engineer and shook his fist, but I doubt the man ever heard or saw him. Grandpa went and looked at Foxy. Then he came down the road and up the lane and into the house, just brushing past me like I wasn't even there. When he came out he had his gun, so I knew poor Foxy wasn't dead yet. I couldn't watch. I went back into the kitchen. It was quiet for so long. Then one shot. After a while your Grandpa came back in and cleaned the gun and put it away. Then he took a spade and buried old Foxy down by the right-of-way. And he's never had another dog about the place, not to this day.''

"Maybe he could have changed his mind." The more impossible it seemed the more I wanted to keep Goldie.

"Oh Blaine, your Uncle Bob's tempted him with puppies many a time. There've been strays around looking for a handout. He just sent them off with a stone at their heels. So you'd better get that one out of sight before he comes in for his supper.''

"She's awful hungry and she's got a sore paw, I think."

Gramma bit her lip. Gramma could never turn down a needy person — or a dog, I reckoned; I was counting on it.

"Well, maybe the end of the roast. There's not much on it but bone. But you take her down to the road to eat it, mind, or she'll think she can stay.''

I grabbed the left-over roast and ran down the lane and round onto the Norwich-Tillsonburg Road, where the ditches were deep and the trees would hide us from the house. Goldie tore into the meat as if she hadn't had a bite in days. I ran my hand down her side. You could feel her ribs all right, but she didn't look too badly off. If she *were* a stray she'd been making out all right on handouts and thefts.

As she ate I began to pick the burrs and twigs and dead leaves out of her fine golden-red hair. Boy, she was a mess. She smelled a bit too, though no worse than a lot of farm dogs. When she'd got rid of the worst of her hunger and was just playfully gnawing at the bone I took a look at her front right paw. The foot was hot and when I turned it over I could see that the pad was swollen.

She whimpered as I struggled to push her toes apart and get out the object — it was a miserable dirty-looking thorn — but she didn't once bare her teeth at me or growl. When I was through she laid her head on my thighs and rolled her eyes up at me. Absentmindedly I began to stroke her small neat head and run my fingers into the thick fur behind her ears.

Clang, clang, clang. That was the bell Gramma used to warn us that supper was ready. But I didn't want to leave Goldie. *Clang, clang.* However, I couldn't stay out here all night and I was hungry. In fact, I was starving. I scrambled to my feet and Goldie pricked up her ears.

"Stay," I told her sternly and she lay as flat as a hearthrug in the ditch. I walked up the road to the corner of the lane. "Stay," I warned her again. Then I hesitated. Suppose she started to wander down the road? There was a lot more traffic these days. Or suppose she were to head along the concession road and a train happened by? She might finish up like Foxy.

I looked back. "Come on then." And she was up, leaping and limping at the same time. "Good dog then." I fondled her silky ears. "Maybe I could hide you under the front porch. Grandpa never goes round the front. I could smuggle you food. Will you stay, Goldie? Will you lie quiet?"

She wagged her feathery tail and looked up at me with her intelligent brown eyes. There was a break in the trellis work that screened the area under the porch, and I showed her where to wriggle through. "Stay! Stay!"

Clang, clang. "BLAINE!" I ran around the house and into the kitchen, stopping just long enough to wash the dog smell off my hands. Grandpa, Greatgramma and Rose and Charlie were already at table and Gramma was starting to dish up.

"What kept you, boy?"

"Sorry, Grandpa," I muttered and tackled my food without another word.

We were halfway through dessert when I heard a faint scratching noise at the front door. I looked quickly around, but no one else seemed to have heard it. After all, there was a closed door and a long passage between the kitchen and the front door. I began to shovel in my pie as fast as I could.

"Manners, manners," screeched Greatgramma and whacked me with the back of her spoon before I could get my knuckles out of the way. She was still every bit as speedy as when I'd first moved in.

The scratching came again. Much louder this time.

"What the tarnation?" Grandpa muttered. He got up and threw open the door between the kitchen and the main hall. Now the scratches and whines were loud enough for everyone to hear.

I kept my eyes on my plate and tried to go on eating, though my throat was choked up with piecrust crumbs. Grandpa's stocking feet thudded down the passage. I could hear him struggling with the front door bolts. Why, I don't believe that door had been opened since

I'd lived there. Weddings and funerals was the custom.

By now the whining had reached a frenzy. There was the squeal of reluctant hinges, the skidding of claws scrabbling over Gramma's polished oak floor, and into the kitchen burst Goldie. She bounded to my side and squatted beside me, her chin on my knee. There was no way on God's green earth that I could pretend the two of us didn't know each other.

"A dog in the house," shrieked Greatgramma. "Get the dirty beast out. Get it out, I say!"

Now, I don't know if it was Grandpa's natural contrariness that worked for Goldie and me at that moment, or if, seeing the two of us sitting together, he remembered what it was like to be thirteen. But at any rate he shut the door to the front of the house with a bang and said, "If you're planning to keep that creature you'd better give it a bath. It stinks!"

That night, after a bath and a rinse in rainwater that made her hair silkier than ever, Goldie slept at the foot of my bed on an old blanket Gramma had dug out for me. When I woke sweating from a nightmare in which I'd taken Susan into a dark wood and lost her there, I sat up and there was Goldie. She raised her head and looked at me. I could see her eyes flash in the moonlight.

"Go to sleep, Goldie," I whispered and lay down again with her comforting weight against my legs.

Next day her foot was real hot and swollen. Gramma showed me how to make hot bread poultices to draw out the poison. I stayed by her all Sunday, changing the poultices as they cooled and stroking her head.

She was a healthy dog, and in a few days the swelling went down and the foot healed properly. But that sore foot was a lucky stroke for both of us, because by the time Goldie could walk without limping she was clearly established as a house dog, with a place of her own on the rag rug in front of the stove and on the old blanket at the foot of my bed.

Grandpa never said one word for or against Goldie. It was almost as if she were invisible. Then one day, after I'd had Goldie for about a month, I surprised him squatting on the path close to the barn fondling her ears and muzzle, while she tried to lick his face. He stood up as soon as he saw me.

"Fool dog got something in her eye," he said and stomped off.

Now, when school was over, I had something to come home to. Rain or dry, Goldie was always waiting for me at the bottom of the lane. On weekends we'd be up at first light and off walking across country till nightfall, when we'd come home and fall exhausted in a heap together in front of the stove, then wolf down Gramma's stew and drop into bed to sleep until morning.

That winter I never seemed to stop eating. I was making up for the lean years, I guess. And I went on growing, though now I was filling in with muscle and my face lost its bony look. The snow came and toboggan time. Goldie loved the snow. She'd jump into drifts, all four feet at once, and scramble out with an idiotic look of surprise on her face. Then she'd do it all over again. Once we'd got the toboggan runs good and smooth she'd skid down them on her front, her tail waving furiously.

She was great with all the other guys, but she made it flatteringly clear that she was my dog, or that I was her person. When snow balled up on her hairy feet or got into lumps between her toes she'd always come to me to have it fixed.

"She must have come from a good family," Gramma

remarked one day. "One with children. She's so gentle with the little ones. I do wonder where she's from…"

"Nowhere," I said sharply. "Nowhere but here."

"Oh, she must have had a home, Blaine. I'm just surprised that no one's come by enquiring."

"No!" I shouted. "You're wrong, I know you are." And I ran out of the house, calling Goldie after me. For a moment I actually hated Gramma. How could she say a thing like that! Goldie was just an old stray, and now she was mine. I smoothed her neat round head and the beautiful golden-red hair that gave me the lie. In my heart I knew Goldie was no stray.

Now I was afraid. The snow was deep that January and I used the weather as an excuse to keep Goldie in the house, except for letting her out in the yard for exercise and fresh air before school and when I got home. Suppose someone should see her who knew who she really was? In the house she was safe.

But the damage had already been done, though I didn't know it at the time. Mrs. Ferguson had talked to her cousin visiting from Woodstock, all about this beautiful golden retriever that her son's friend owned. When her cousin went home she happened to mention it to a neighbour. So, down the line from mouth to ear to mouth the story of Goldie went, until one breezy March day, when the ditches were full of melting snow, a car pulled up at the bottom of our lane.

I was helping Gramma hang out the sheets and Goldie was playing her game of snapping at, but never actually biting, the flapping corners of the sheets. We turned to stare at the couple in front and the three kids piled in the back.

The man climbed out and began to walk up our lane.

"Hey there, Jenny!" he suddenly called, and Gramma opened her mouth to tell him he'd made a mistake, that she was Maggie Cameron. But Goldie shivered right down her spine. She raced towards the man and ran around and around him. Then she galloped down to where the car was parked on the concession road.

I stood there with my mouth open, watching my Goldie leaping and licking and moaning in her throat, and the kids falling out of the car and crying and hugging her and yelling: "Jenny, Jenny!" What a dumb name for a dog, I thought dully. There was no need for argument or proof as to whose dog she really was. I left them talking in the lane and bolted across the wet fields to the sugar bush at the back.

The bush was full of the tiny sounds of maple sap plinking into the cans and the louder sounds of birds shouting at each other from the brush. I heard Goldie bark, just once, like she was saying goodbye maybe. Maybe not. She'd never looked back at me, just high-tailed it down the lane. Well, why should she? She owed me nothing. It was she who'd given me all that loving.

A car started up. I heard the gears grind. Then there was just the plink of the sap in the cans. I trudged back to the house through the melting snow.

"They were real polite," Gramma reported. "They even offered to pay for Goldie's keep."

"But you didn't take anything, did you?" I asked fiercely.

"Of course I didn't, Blaine. The very idea!"

That was all that was said about Goldie. The old blanket stayed on the bottom of my bed, smelling faintly of dog, until the warm weather came and Gramma washed all the bedding and stored it away again.

They didn't offer to get me another dog. I'd thought they would, and I was steeling myself against it. I didn't want to. Not ever.

Not long after, Dad came to the farm for a rare visit. I had begun to understand that seeing me just reminded him of Mom, and that was something he couldn't bear, which was why he left me pretty much to Grandpa and Gramma. But this Sunday near the middle of April he arrived, getting a lift up from a neighbour. And he'd brought me a bicycle. It was store-new, bright blue, with sturdy wheels and handlebars.

"I know your birthday's not for another month, but it's a pity not to take advantage of the spring weather. By summer you'll be so busy with the tobacco you'll have no spare time. So here it is." It was one of the longest speeches I'd heard him make.

"Dad!" I ran my hands lovingly over the shining frame. "It's super! But can you afford it? Really? I could help if you like. Gramma's got my tobacco money saved."

"Nope. It's your birthday. That's an end of it." He shifted from foot to foot, looking anxious, as if he were about to take off again.

"You can stay the day, can't you? The whole day?" And Gramma came out and persuaded him at least to come into the house and sit down for midday dinner.

It was almost like the old times, I thought. If only Mom had been there, sitting beside him.

Greatgramma must have read my thoughts because right then she piped up, "See anything of that flighty wife of yours, Ed?" Then she sat back, her black eyes snapping, waiting.

Dad went white. Then two red spots flared in his cheeks. He got up from the table.

"I don't believe I'll stay for dinner, Mrs. Cameron. Thank you kindly, but I just dropped by to see the boy."

I ran after him down the lane.

"Stay for dinner, *please*. Don't pay attention to Greatgramma. She's crazy."

He shook his head. He was such a quiet man, almost invisible. When he was gone I didn't even think about him that much. Grandpa and Gramma filled my life. But it shouldn't be that way. Now he was going to walk down the road away from me again. Like Goldie. I couldn't bear for him to go like that.

"Thanks for the bike. It's great. Really."

"That's all right."

"Dad!" I wanted to pull him back to me. To hold onto him. But I didn't know how. I struggled for words. Why was it so hard?

"Dad, I...I love you."

"Thank you, son," he said, real quiet. But he flinched, like I'd hit him instead of telling him I loved him. He walked very fast the rest of the way down the lane and turned onto the road to Tillsonburg.

He was much shorter than I was, I suddenly realized, with a stoop in his shoulders I didn't remember. And his fine fair hair was going thin on top where there had once been a thick thatch.

A car came by and stopped to pick him up. I stood at the bottom of the lane staring along the dusty road. He didn't *want* my love. He didn't want anyone's love.

I struggled with this idea. Slowly I began to understand that after Mom had hurt him, not just the once when she left, but over and over again up till that last moment, he wasn't going to let himself be hurt by anyone ever again. Even if he had to shut out the whole world to shut out the pain.

That's crazy, I thought angrily. *You can't do that. You might as well be dead.*

A train rattled across the level crossing on the

134

concession road behind me and made me jump. I
turned and walked slowly back to the house. Hadn't I
behaved that way after Susan's death? And wasn't I
about to repeat the same pattern now that Goldie'd
been taken from me?

"No I won't," I said aloud over the noise of the train.
"I'm going to live even if it hurts."

I rode my bike to school and it opened up a new world.
A dozen or more of us got into the habit of biking
around the countryside in the evenings as the days
grew longer. Once the tobacco was growing I was hired
on again for suckering, but as soon as the Saturday's
work was done the gang would head off for the swimming hole about five miles east of the farm.

I don't think there's a greater pleasure in the world
than skinning out of stiff and sweaty clothes and
bounding stark naked down a grassy slope and into the
water. The spring that fed the swimming hole was like
ice and the water was very deep; it never warmed up
till the end of July.

We used to scream and thrash around and crawl out
with blue toes and lips, shivering and goosefleshed, to
warm up and then plunge in again. We'd stay until it
began to grow dark, when we'd shake ourselves dry,
scramble back into our dirty clothes and bike westward
into the sunset until we came to the highway.

Back home I'd wolf down the supper that Gramma
kept warm for me and then I'd drag off my clothes and
fall into bed, my skin cool and clean, to plunge into
deep and dreamless sleep. That was the way I exorcised
Susan and Goldie.

As I learned to stop feeling sorry for myself, I
realized that the Senior Fourth exams weren't too far
ahead. Then I was going to have to make a choice.

What was I going to do with my life? The farm was a far-off promise of Grandpa's. Till then...?

"I presume you're going to High School," Miss Kenworth, the Senior Fourth teacher, said one day.

"I don't know..."

"You're not sixteen yet, are you? You *have* to stay in school till you're sixteen. And your marks are excellent, especially in English. It won't cost that much..."

"You mean we have to *pay*?"

"There'll be books, of course, and since you live outside the township line there'll be a fee as well."

"I don't know about that," I said, thinking of Grandpa.

"Would you like to have me talk to your family?"

"No. No, thanks." Grandpa could eat Miss Kenworth up and spit out the pieces if he was in the mood. "I'll talk to them."

The opportunity came a few evenings later.

"So you'll be through school in another month, eh?"

"Just public school, Grandpa."

"Eight grades is more than enough for a farmer. I only had two years of school and I've done just fine."

Gramma jumped in to help.

"Things are different now, Alistair. Most of the children go on, at least to First and Second Form. Wouldn't you like to see Blaine get his Junior Matriculation?"

"Don't see why."

"Miss Kenworth says I should go on. She says my marks are all right, especially in English."

"*English*? Well, it's your own language, ain't it?"

"Yes, Grandpa."

"Can you read and write and spell good?"

"Yes, Grandpa."

"Then what in the tarnation world do you want any more 'English' for?" His face was starting to get red.

Suppose he refuses to let me go? I thought. He might be sent to jail. It was the law, Miss Kenworth had said. Till I was sixteen.

"It won't cost that much," I pleaded.

"You mean I'm supposed to *pay* for you to go to school for four more years to go on learning your mother tongue? Well, I always said the government was crazy, but this about takes the cake, it does."

Grandpa's face got so red that the old scars showed up like pale threads. In her rocker by the stove Greatgramma chuckled and stirred. In a minute she'd come up with something so outrageous that Grandpa would overstep himself and not be able to back down.

"That's okay, Grandpa," I said. "I don't care that much anyway." As I went out I saw Greatgramma pouting as if I'd snatched away a piece of her favourite peppermint candy.

Did I care? The only thing that really mattered was getting away. Could I do it better with eight grades of education or with twelve? It looked pretty hopeless either way.

I cut down on the bike riding and studied for the exams. I couldn't believe that they were this soon. With less exercise I found I couldn't manage a third helping of pie at supper.

"What's the matter, boy? You sickening for something?"

"No, Grandpa, thanks. I'm fine."

"He's grieving because he can't go to High School," Gramma suggested.

Grandpa snorted.

"No, it's all right, Gramma. I understand. Grandpa really *does* need my help on the farm. After all, he's getting on. I should be..."

"Getting on?" Grandpa went purple from his neck

to the top of his head. "Getting *on*? Why, I can still do the work of two of you, with one hand tied behind my back."

"Well, then, what's holding you back from letting Blaine go to High School?" Gramma put in sharply.

That held Grandpa for a minute. It wasn't like Gramma to attack head on.

"If you want to know, it's the idea of having to *pay* for his schooling that sticks in my craw. While the Blounts and the Amerys don't have to."

"They live inside the township line, Grandpa."

"Well, I know that, boy. I'm not stupid."

"So they pay town taxes and you don't."

"And they get the fire brigade out when their barns catch fire. And I don't. That's worth what they pay in taxes, I reckon."

"I tell you what," Gramma said suddenly. "If it's just the money holding you back, suppose we let Blaine pay for his books and his schooling out of his tobacco money? If he does that, you surely won't object to paying his keep for the next four years?"

"What about his clothes? He's growing like a weed."

The conversation went on as if I wasn't there. I opened my mouth to say it didn't matter, that I wasn't crazy about more school if Grandpa could make it all right with the truant officer, when Gramma chimed in again.

"There's more than enough saved for nice clothes. You won't need to be ashamed of him."

"Waste of money, waste of money!" Greatgramma piped up, and for the first time in my life I agreed with her. What could I say? I wanted to yell: *That's my money. My escape money. You can't touch that.* But how could I? Grandpa and Gramma had given me everything: a home, food, clothes, loving. In return I'd done precious little more than a few chores.

So I sat in silence while Grandpa allowed himself to be persuaded. I took the exams and my marks were up in the eighties. In the fall of 1938 Gramma and I went into town to buy my clothes and books; and Gramma took my money and traded it for my higher education.

Now I'll *never* get away, I thought gloomily. When the little bit of money was left was safely back in Gramma's green tin box and my new clothes were neatly folded in the drawers of my bureau, I grabbed my bike and took off, pounding the pedals up the hills, coasting down the valleys, trying to escape from my helpless anger.

I biked farther than ever before, as far as Cornell, and got there just as one of the passenger trains went by. I stood beside the right-of-way with my hands clutching the handlebars of my bike, feeling the familiar shake of the ground beneath my feet, smelling the heady smell of hot metal and oil and coal soot.

Stop! I yelled inside myself. *Stop this one time and let me aboard.*

Then the train was gone. The line was empty. I looked along the concession road towards the sleepy village. It was even smaller than I had remembered. Someone *had* bought our farm. Someone was living in *our* house. There was washing on the line and smoke coming from the chimney. The house looked smaller. Even the great mulberry tree seemed to have shrunk.

Was all life a cheat? Even the past was not what I remembered. No wonder Dad had left Grandpa's for a job in Tillsonburg. He'd known from the day we left that there wasn't a hope of our ever getting the farm back. Maybe he didn't really *want* it. Maybe he was tired of the backbreak and the heartbreak, and that's why he'd given up without more of a fight.

I turned away from the farm and the railway. As my

bike gained speed and the wind whipped through my sweaty hair, I remembered that day at the Ex, the roller coaster and the Ferris Wheel. And Mom.

Had I really seen her there that day? My memory of the farm and the mulberry tree had shrunk to a poor and meagre reality. Had Mom *really* been at the Ex?

But she *had* escaped. That part was real.

Could I do the same thing? Gramma had used my escape money for my education, because she loved me and she thought that was what I wanted. But she'd done more than that. She'd made me realize their goodness to me that was like a weight on my fourteen-year-old shoulders. I owed them everything. How *could* I get away?

I peddled furiously away from my thoughts, wishing that I could escape into an airplane like John, shucking off gravity and the weight of responsibility with it.

EIGHT

Many of my friends went on to High School, so it wasn't as bad as I had expected. The principal, Mr. McReady, was a stocky man with a waxed moustache and hair parted in the middle and smoothed down with oil. He always wore a black suit with a vest, summer and winter, and it was always greyed over with a bloom of chalk dust. He didn't use the strap much, but he had the deadliest aim with the blackboard eraser of anyone I'd ever met. If he'd been a baseball player I reckon he'd have been on the cigarette cards with Babe Ruth and Walter Johnson and the rest. His subject was Math, and I figured if I was careful I wouldn't have any trouble with Mr. McReady.

My problem turned out to be something quite unexpected. It was a girl. Her name was Maud Forsythe. I'd noticed her around in Junior and Senior Fourth, but I'd never paid her no mind, nor she me. She was the kind of girl who'd wrinkle up her nose at the smell of a barn and faint clean away at a dollop of horse manure. Her hair was in ringlets and she wore fussy dresses to school. Her father was the bank manager and Grandpa said he'd done all right for himself.

For some reason Maud just wouldn't leave me alone. Her desk was right next to mine, and I was sorry for that the very first day. She kept whispering and trying to pass me dumb notes. I pretended I couldn't hear or see her, but that just seemed to make her more anxious.

"Ask me to the movies Saturday, Blaine."

Silence.

"Oh, come on. We'll have such a good time."

Silence.

"Blaine!"

"Why don't you hush up?" I hissed. Then, *wham*, the wooden side of the eraser caught me full on the forehead. It hurt like heck and there was chalk dust in my eyes and hair, not to mention all over my desk. As I took the eraser back to Mr. McReady the girls giggled behind their hands, but I noticed some of the guys were looking sympathetic. I guess they knew Maud.

At recess I went right up to her and told her to stop bugging me. That was a real mistake.

"Take me to the movies Saturday and I won't."

"I work Saturdays."

"Oh, come on. Tobacco's finished. And you don't work nights."

I hesitated.

"Come on. You scared to take a girl out?"

"Course not. Well, maybe I'll take you once. If you stop bugging me in class."

"Great! Meet you outside the theatre Saturday evening." She ran off with her ringlets tossing, and I saw her talking to her friends with a real smug expression, just as if I'd asked her instead of being practically blackmailed.

I got a real razzing at home when I explained why I'd be out late on Saturday.

"Better watch yourself," Grandpa warned. "You're a bit young to be going out with the ladies."

"Just make sure you wear your suit, not your overalls," Rose advised.

"And see your fingernails are clean. And your ears," Gramma added.

"Gee, Gramma, she's not going to be looking at my ears and that. Anyway, it'll be dark in there."

Then they all started laughing like crazy and I could feel my face getting red.

Come Saturday Gramma sponged and pressed my school suit and gouged out my nails with a sharpened match stick.

"Gramma, stop! Ouch, you're hurting!"

"You wouldn't want her to think you were a savage, would you?"

Actually I wouldn't have minded a bit; putting Maud off would be a relief, but I didn't want everyone at home to know that I'd been pressured into going. So I smiled and said goodbye and buttoned up my jacket — there was a mean wind that evening — and biked into town and locked my bike in the lane beside the movie house.

There was a line outside already, and Jock and Arnie yelled at me.

"Hey, didn't know you were coming. Sit with us."

"I can't," I muttered, real low. "I'm meeting someone."

"He can come too. The more the better. We're going to sit right up front. It looks like fun."

It was a movie called *The Mummy*, with Boris Karloff, all wrapped up in bandages on the poster outside, like Grandpa after the Toonerville Trolley got him, only a whole lot skinnier.

"It's a girl," I muttered, even lower, so none of the other guys would hear. Then I bolted to the back of the line. Pretty soon they opened the movie house and the line began to move along, but no sign of Maud. I began to hope: *Maybe her parents hadn't let her go out.* Soon it was my turn and Maud still hadn't arrived.

I stood in the freezing wind wondering whether to

buy a single now I was here, or go off home and save my money. Just then Maud came tittupping along the street.

"Oh, I *do* hope I didn't keep you waiting!"

I bought two tickets and grabbed her arm and pulled her inside. We were so late that all the front seats were taken and we had to make do with two right at the back among all the necking couples. *Oh lord*, I thought, and slumped as far down in my seat as I could, hoping none of my friends would look back and see me.

There was a Donald Duck cartoon, which was great, and a news reel about this man Hitler at a place called Munich, and how there was going to be peace because of something Chamberlain had done. It was kind of boring.

Then the movie began, and I forgot about Maud. It was all about this mummy coming alive when the man who'd been digging up these graves read a special curse out loud. It was real spooky when the mummy's hand came out, all stiff with rotten-looking bandages around it, and snatched the paper out of the man's hand.

Right at that moment Maud let out an awful scream, which just about scared the pants off me, and flung herself across me and buried her head in my chest. She wouldn't come up for air for about five minutes.

"Is it all right? Can I look now?" she kept asking. I just batted her ringlets out of my face so I could see and concentrated on the screen.

Maud had trapped my right arm against the chair and it was getting pins and needles something fierce. After a time I managed to wriggle it free and drape it around her shoulder; well, there wasn't anywhere else to put it. I felt stupid and looked around casually to see if anyone else had noticed, but most of the couples near us were sitting like that anyway.

After a time, when the action slowed down for a minute or so, I noticed that Maud's hair smelled nice under my chin, and her wool sweater was kind of soft against me — she'd taken off her coat before flinging herself around.

Then the movie turned exciting again. The young scientist, the one who hadn't gone crazy, was trying to rescue the girl that the dead mummy was in love with. In the end the girl was saved and the mummy got burned up, so I suppose it really was dead this time. I thought it was kind of a pity. It'd have been a lot more interesting if Boris Karloff could have killed the girl, the way he wanted to; then the two of them would have been mummies, going on scaring everyone to death. But it was a terrific show in spite of the soppy ending.

The lights went up and I pushed Maud off my chest and helped her into her coat. It was really dark outside and I knew Gramma would expect me to see her home, so I set off beside her. It was freezing cold with just a jacket on, and all I wanted to do was to get rid of Maud, have a pee and bike home; but she strolled along as if it was the middle of July, talking about the movie. From the things she'd thought interesting you'd have sworn we'd been seeing two different shows.

Finally we came to this house with a tall dark hedge around it.

"I'll go the rest of the way by myself, thank you, Blaine," she said suddenly and unhitched herself from my arm.

"Okay!" I said. What a relief.

"Thank you so much for a delightful evening," she went on, real affected, and stood so close to me that she had to look up to see my face and her silly ringlets hung way down the back of her coat.

"That's okay," I said again and stepped back, just as

a tall skinny man leaped out of an opening in the hedge behind Maud. Right after seeing that movie, just for a moment I thought...anyway I let out a yell, and Maud screeched and flung herself on my chest.

It was Mr. Forsythe, of course, as I could see when I was over my surprise.

"Unhand my daughter, young man," he said.

I tried to explain that I wasn't handing her; on the contrary I'd been trying to leave, but he didn't let me get a word in edgeways. Words just poured out of him like a spring run-off, stuff out of the Bible about the temptations of the flesh.

When he stopped for breath at last I said, "Gee, Mr. Forsythe, it was only a movie, and I brought Maud right home. I didn't know you'd an objection to the movies."

He peered at me. It was quite dark and the great hedge looming over us didn't help.

"It's Blaine Williams, isn't it? Know your grandfather. He wouldn't let you get up to any shenanigans, I'll be bound."

"No, sir," I said fast.

"Off you go. Don't let me see you around here again. As for you, Miss..."

I turned and ran ignobly down the road, leaving him shaking Maud by the shoulders, going on all the time about hellfire. I saw a few lace curtains twitch as I ran by, and I was thankful to get out of the neighbourhood, go back to the movie house to pick up my bike, and ride home.

I felt horribly guilty at having abandoned Maud, but I needn't have. The very next recess I saw her making up to Harry Gates, so she didn't bug me again, for which I was thankful.

Midway through the next term she stopped coming to school at all, and shortly after that Harry left. The next we knew they were married, there was a baby on the way and Harry was working in his Dad's hardware store.

There was a lot of gossip about Maud's behaviour, and the whole affair worried me, so I went down the road to talk it over with John. He was the only person I *could* talk to about stuff like that. Grandpa and Gramma were too old, and I never had that kind of family feeling about Charlie, for all he'd been married to Aunt Rose for four years. He was okay, but I couldn't trust him not to tell Rose.

When I told John about Maud he laughed till I thought he'd bust.

"Boy, you were lucky to escape alive. Let that be a warning to you not to deal with that kind of girl."

"But why did she go after *me*? There were lots of other guys to pick from."

"Guess you haven't noticed yourself in the mirror recently. You were an awfully scrawny kid, but you've filled out some. You're not such a bad-looking fellow — the sort the girls seem to go for."

That was a little scary. I wasn't ready for girls yet. I could see that they might be another kind of trap. Look what had happened to Harry.

"What'll I *do*?"

"Well, if there's no one you're really keen on, the smartest thing to do would be to pick out a real quiet girl and go steady with her till you're through school. That way you'll be safe from the other kind."

"And then ditch her, you mean?"

"Yup. You've got your own life to lead."

I walked slowly back to the farm, thinking. In my room I stared at my face in the silvery spotted mirror. I *had* changed since I'd last taken a good look at myself back after Susie's death. My face had filled out and my shoulders were broader. My skin had tanned a golden brown and my mousy hair had sunbleached near blond from all the summer days in the tobacco fields.

"Admiring your charms?"

I jumped. Aunt Rose was leaning against the door post, smiling in that slightly insulting way she still had. Marriage to Charlie had softened her some, but she was still Aunt Rose. I blushed.

"Course not. Something John said. I guess I've put on weight." I brushed past her and went down to help Gramma with the chores.

Next Monday I took a look around at the girls in First Form. There were three or four really dull ones, the sort that kept their eyes on their desk and answered in whispers and huddled in the corner of the school-yard during recess.

Really, I'd be doing one of them a favour, I told myself, and I'd just about narrowed my choice down when I had a vision of myself, sitting on a stump in the sugar bush, crying my eyes out after Susan's death.

It was weird. I could hear the faint plink of the sap in the buckets and smell the clean scent of melting snow. And I could remember every word of the promise I'd made Susan that day.

I was pretty well disgusted at myself. I was using people again. John was four years older than me, and my very best friend, but I knew that this time he'd been wrong.

What I did was to start working part-time in the broom factory in Norwich. It kept me out of trouble and it meant more money. Even though I couldn't see how I was ever going to escape the obligation of Grandpa's goodness to me and his promise of the farm, I did feel more powerful, more as if escape was *possible*, when I had money stored in Gramma's green tin box.

It was Charlie who helped me get the job, and after a couple of days at it I marvelled that he'd hung on all those years before coming to work for us and marrying Rose. It was a terrible job.

The factory was in a large warehouse, and the first thing that hit me was the noise. The corn fibres came into the factory in great bales and had to be fed into a shredder that cut them all the right width to make bristles. My job was to stand at a broom-making machine, grab a handful of heavy corn for the centre, surround it with two layers of shredded stuff for the outside, then slap the metal cover around the broom handle, which was held in a vice, so that it covered the ends of the fibres. A foot pedal brought down the wire, the handle spun around, wrapping the wire around the handle, fastening the corn fibre to it. A fast slash with a knife trimmed the upper ends and then I had to toss the broom into a box to go to the stitcher.

The stitchers worked at heavy machines that pounded the fibres flat and stitched through them to hold them in place. When the shredders, the broom-makers and the sewing machines were all going full tilt you couldn't hear yourself think, and the air was filled with dirt and corn dust. Any time there was a lull in the noise you could hear people coughing.

The owner made us pay for our own knives, which I thought was unfair, since we were only paid twenty cents for every dozen brooms. Sometimes the corn would come in damp and you'd have to be extra careful wrapping the good stuff around the outside so it wouldn't all fall apart. At times the smell was so sickening that it would stay in my nostrils all the way home and I could taste it clean through Gramma's chicken stew and dumplings.

Charlie'd lost the top two joints of his index finger

in the broom machine. It was easy to do. That wire spinning around the rotating broom handle could cut through flesh as easy as a hot knife through butter. But I stuck to the job through that winter, from right after school till six on weekdays and from eight in the morning until six on Saturdays. My hands grew calloused and skilful. Slowly, very slowly, my escape fund began to grow again.

Then spring came and the tender tobacco seedlings were set out in the fields. I used to bike down to Van Hoosan's farm on Sundays and watch the lush leaves grow, waiting for the day when it was time to start suckering and I could quit the broom factory and move out into the fresh air.

I guess everything's relative. After a couple of days' suckering, with the sun pounding on my shoulders and my back breaking and my nostrils full of the sticky bitter smell, I'd think I was badly off. Then I'd have to remind myself of the grind, slash, pound and thunk of the broom factory, to know I was much better off outside.

On June 7th, just around the start of suckering, the King and Queen came to Woodstock. They were on their way back from a trip across Canada, but they were stopping in Woodstock just for *us*. The whole school went up and waited on the stands, with all the schools from the other towns round about, for the royal train to arrive. There were bands and red, white and blue bunting, and each of us had a small Union Jack to wave.

The air was just jumping with excitement. Sometimes there'd be a sudden lull and you could hear the quiet ting-ting of the telegraph over in the station. Then the bands would start banging and tooting away again, everyone's voice would join together to make a roar that was different from anything I'd ever heard. It wasn't like the crowd at the CNE, where thousands of people were all enjoying themselves separately. That day at Woodstock, it was more as if this huge crowd were a single creature.

There were false alarms, and all heads craned to see. Then something stupid would happen, like a dog trotting across the square to lift its leg against the decorated stand, and everyone would roar with laughter.

Finally the real train arrived, with the King and Queen on a platform at the rear. There was a moment's silence, as if no one could quite believe it, and the bands, more or less together, struck up "God Save the King." The King and Queen came out of the station and walked across the square to be greeted by the Mayor and talk to people lined up to meet them. The Queen waved up at us kids and we waved our flags and shouted till we were hoarse.

It seemed no time at all till they went back on the train, which had been sitting with full steam up all this time. They waved from the rear platform as the train pulled out and we waved back until the train was out of sight. But I thought for a long time about that train, travelling across Ontario, stitching together all the little communities into a single patchwork.

Just before final exams that year I got to know Nancy Black. What with classes and homework, farm chores and jobs, there wasn't much time left except for eating and sleeping. But this day I was in the school library during lunch hour looking up something for a history project, and I couldn't help noticing her. I mean noticing her in a different way from just the skinny girl with reddish brown braids and freckles who sat ahead of me in class.

She was sitting at the table in the middle of the

library, her thin legs wound around the chair legs, her elbows on the table and her hands over her ears. She didn't even look up when I dumped a load of books on the far end of the table.

The only time she moved at all, apart from her eyes, was when her right hand would turn the page and then go up to cover her ear again. After a while I began to get real nosy about what she was reading that was so special, but her book was too far away for me to read the title upside down.

I'd just about finished my assignment when the bell went for afternoon school. I hurriedly finished my notes and tidied my books. Nancy didn't even budge. She sat at the table as if she'd been carved out of a hunk of rock. I nudged her and her face came up, blank and kind of dazed. She had the strangest green eyes I'd ever seen.

"Huh?"

"Time for class."

She blinked and stretched and followed me out of the library and back to class without a word. At afternoon recess I latched on to her.

"What were you reading?"

"*The Count of Monte Cristo*." She hesitated and then went on in a rush. "I've just got to where he's sewing himself up in the sack so they'll think he's the corpse of the old man, but I don't see how he's *ever* going to get out. I'm sure he'll drown when they throw him in the sea."

"It's okay. He..."

"Don't tell me. Don't tell." Her voice went up.

I grinned. She reminded me so much of myself a couple of years before.

"All right. But you'll love it. Have you read *Lorna Doone*?"

"Not yet. But I just finished *Coral Island*. It was

horrible though, when the poor natives got squished under the canoe. I stopped liking it then."

We plunged into books until the bell rang.

"I don't understand why you spend your lunchtimes reading. Why don't you take books home?"

"Oh, I couldn't," was all she would say. I found out later that she was the oldest of a family of harum-scarum boys who'd as soon throw a book in the manure pile for a joke as not.

"If only I could buy my own. I'd hide them in a special secret place."

"Don't you have any money for books?"

She shook her head.

"Ma buys my clothes out of the egg money, and she'll let me buy wool to knit presents for the family, but there's never enough for anything as frivolous as a book."

I hadn't thought until then how much luckier I was to be a boy, to work and have money of my own for school and clothes and books, if I wanted.

"You're welcome to come over to our place on Sunday. I've got a trunk full of books belonging to my Dad. We've got *Lorna Doone*, and *The Man in the Iron Mask* and *The Scarlet Pimpernel*."

She went so white with excitement that all her freckles stood out as if they'd been painted on her nose and cheeks. She looked so like a Raggedy Ann doll that I wanted to laugh.

"Really?" she whispered.

"Sure."

"I wouldn't dare borrow anything. But if we could just read, once in a while, and talk about books. I wouldn't be a nuisance."

"Of course you wouldn't."

I made sure that she'd come over for midday dinner the very next Sunday. Her father's farm was off the

Woodstock Road, so I biked across town to pick her up and bring her home, balanced on the crossbar of my bike.

The time we shared that summer, talking about books, escaping into the world of Cavaliers and Roundheads, of D'Artagnan and the Cardinal, was like the still point at the centre of a hurricane. Outside things were beginning to change. On the surface there was just the haying and the wheat and oats and tobacco. But beyond our everyday life, it was as if a great clock were ticking.

Everyone was talking about the news from Europe. People tended to keep the radio on all day. It was our only connection with the world.

Then on September 3rd the clock struck. We woke up to a fine fall Sunday and the news that Britain was at war with Germany.

"Of course we'll join in," some people said.

"But it's not *our* war. It's Europe's," said others.

Then the civilian liner Athenia was torpedoed off the coast of Ireland by a Nazi submarine, and among the dead was a ten-year-old girl from Hamilton, Ontario. That made people mad.

"Wish Mackenzie King would get off his royal butt," Grandpa said, and that was the politest comment.

The very next Sunday we heard over the radio that Canada had also declared war on Germany. Right after dinner that afternoon John came over to see us. His eyes were sparkling and he couldn't sit still for a moment.

"We're off to join the air force," he said. "Matt Thurman and I."

"Who's Matt Thurman? Don't recollect the name."

"He's from Tillsonburg, Grandpa. We took flying lessons together."

"But what's your hurry?" Charlie asked. "Nothing's

been set up yet. It'll be months before they'll be ready to recruit."

John shook his head.

"One way or another we're getting into the scrap. We're leaving for Trenton in the morning. If they don't want us we'll just make our way to England somehow and join the RAF. We've both got our licences and we've done a bit of aerobatics. They'll be wanting fighter pilots, I bet you."

"But whatever does your mother think about all this?"

John's face closed up.

"Oh, you know mothers..." He jumped to his feet for the fourth time. "I must go. I've got to pack and get organized. Not that I've much to take." He laughed. "Walk me down the road, Blaine?"

It was a glorious day, on the edge between summer and fall, with the leaves barely beginning to turn colour, so that the green shaded into the gold and orange and the trees looked extra round and lush. The harvest was in, but the fields hadn't been ploughed over yet, and the stubble shone silver.

John stopped, where the road went atop a little rise, and looked round. He took a deep breath and let it out in a sigh.

"I'll never forget this." I could see his eyes, as fierce as if he were trying to grab every particle of that day and store it in his memory.

"What about the farm, John? What does your father say?"

"Oh, well, Bill's coming along; he's twelve now. And Liz and Peggy are no slouches. If anything should happen to me they can decide between them who's to have the farm. In the meantime there are plenty of hands."

He said it so casually that I didn't catch on for a

minute. When I did I stared at him, the skin suddenly tight across my face. He laughed at my expression.

"That's what war's about, isn't it? Killing."

"But...but you're *jumping* into it. Aren't you scared?"

"Sure. But it's my only way out of here, Blaine. And to fly for a living, which is what I've dreamed of, you know."

"But what about the killing part?"

"I just don't know how I'll feel about that until I'm in it. But we've got to be rid of that Hitler guy, that's for sure. And maybe, up there..." His voice faded as he stared up into that Ontario September blue. "Maybe up there it'll be cleaner. Like a duel, you know. Me against him."

That I could understand. Hadn't I read and re-read *The Three Musketeers* and *The Prisoner of Zenda*? Sword against sword. Skill pitted against cunning. Yes!

"I wish I were old enough," I said. "Gee, by the time I'm nineteen it'll all be over and forgotten, and I'll have missed the chance."

"Yeah, I guess I'm lucky. There's no way it'll last longer than a year. That's why Matt and I want to take off right away. We'll need training, you see. I don't know, maybe three months? It'll be spring before we'll really be involved. By this time next year we'll have wiped that Hitler guy off the map."

We walked slowly to the bottom of the lane leading to John's farm. I stared at John, thinking of the bike rides, of the backbreak of suckering tobacco, row after row, side by side; of the quiet way he'd stood up for me when I was a snotty-nosed kid in Junior Second.

"I'll miss you," I managed to say before my throat tightened up on me.

Then our arms were around each other and we

hugged and beat with our fists on each other's back, as if to prove that this moment was real, that we were alive. And that we loved each other, though there was no possible way of saying it in words.

He drew back and tapped me under the chin with his fist.

"Keep me posted, will ya?" Then he turned up the lane.

"You too," I said to his back. I stood scuffing the stones with my boots till he reached the farmhouse. Then I walked slowly home, feeling that a whole page of my life had just been turned.

It was tough settling into school that fall. The top class was almost empty. More than half the guys had already taken the bus to London to enlist. Some, like Joe Pratt, who was so short-sighted he was almost blind, were sent home again, but the rest were absorbed into the slowly organizing military machine, and weren't seen again until they came home on leave, looking strangely grown-up, in their bulky khaki battledress.

The First Division, which contained Norwich boys, arrived in Scotland just before Christmas. After that you couldn't go into a store without finding at least one mother, a blue letter in her hand, telling the latest news.

"Harry says it's awful. They're in this huge barracks that are just about falling to pieces, and they're freezing to death and the food is terrible."

The smart storekeepers put up little signs on the counters and in their windows: *Buy canned goods for overseas parcels here*.

Gramma came back from shopping in a temper.

"They say there's going to be a shortage of sugar and they won't let me have more than a couple of pounds. Why, I've been buying my sugar in fifty-pound sacks for the last forty years. Sam Small should know I'm not about to start hoarding, but how does he expect me to put up any more applesauce without sugar? Does the Government want them apples to go to waste?"

Right through the winter and the following spring nothing much happened except for rumours and dismal letters from the guys over in England. Lots of girls left town to work in munitions factories, where they were paid big money. Suddenly there were crowds in the stores, because people had money to spend. Hamburger went up from thirteen cents to fifteen cents a pound, and there were rumours that if the war went on for more than a year costs would go out of sight. Already the army was bidding up the price on wheat and meat and vegetables.

I'd seen men playing chess. Sitting staring at the board for hours, very boring to watch. Then suddenly, bam, bam! The first man moves a piece. The second takes it. The first man retaliates and then the game takes off. It was like that in the spring of 1940. The Nazis had taken Denmark and Norway. Then they invaded Belgium, Luxembourg, France! Bam, bam. But unlike the chess game it all seemed pretty one-sided.

A few weeks after my sixteenth birthday the radio announced, as if it were a great victory, that the British Expeditionary Force had got safely back from France, from a little seaside village called Dunkirk. It seemed that every fisherman and boat owner in England had sailed across the Channel and plucked the Army boys off the beach. The newsmen made it sound like a great romantic adventure and everyone got pretty excited. But then we heard that, all the time it was going on, our Canadian boys had been stuck in Aldershot learning how to become soldiers, and we felt let down and mad.

France surrendered and Britain stood alone. I remembered John's guess that it would all be over in a year. Was he right? If he was, would we win? Or would the Nazis end up owning all of Europe? I used to say a prayer before I got into bed at night, mostly for John, and for all the other guys over there too. But I always ended it with: "Please God, don't let the war be over till I have a crack at it."

John's letters became really lively for a couple of months; I could read the excitement between the lines. Then again they became fewer and fewer, with nothing much in them except that he was okay. Later we found out that the Luftwaffe, which was the German Air Force, had started bombing Britain, so I guess John and the other fighter pilots were pretty busy and weren't allowed to say anything.

We had a splendid year on the farm, two hay crops before August and a lot of top quality wheat and oats. There was certainly no trouble finding a market those days, top dollar too. Over Rose's tearful objections Charlie volunteered for the army, but they turned him down. The index finger that he lost in the broom factory probably saved his life. Grandpa was certainly thankful for it; help on the farms was getting hard to come by. Four, five years before, men were beating a path to our door asking for work. Not even for pay, just for a bed and three square meals a day, back when it was hardly worth while putting in a crop, it fetched so little.

"Farming's a crazy business," said Grandpa.

As soon as school was over and the harvest was safely in I caught the bus down to London and volunteered for the army. I might be only sixteen, but I was in a darn sight better shape than a lot of the men there, with bad teeth, and ribs and backbones sticking out of their skin from all those years when there wasn't enough to eat. I was almost six feet tall, a hundred and sixty pounds of muscle without an ounce of flab.

But when the recruiting sergeant asked to see my birth certificate I knew I hadn't a chance. I thought they'd just take my word for it, but the sergeant grinned and said, "Nice try, sonny. Come back when you're nineteen."

Nineteen! That was three years away. By then it was *bound* to be over. I thought about it on the bus back to Norwich and made a plan. I managed to filch my birth certificate out of Gramma's green tin box without her seeing and smuggle it up to my room.

I scraped with the fine blade of my penknife at the crossbar and down stroke of the 4 in 1924 until I'd turned it into a passable 1. It looked a bit obvious, but I rubbed my thumb over the paper until it was all pretty grubby, and then I swear you couldn't tell what I'd done without a magnifying glass.

I went back to London, praying I wouldn't meet up with the same recruiting sergeant, or that if I did he wouldn't remember me. I was in luck. The guy across the desk took my particulars and then asked for the certificate. I fished it out of my overalls pocket, where I'd been carrying it for a couple of days. He unfolded it gingerly.

"Geez, what d'you do with this, eat off it? That's an important document, you know."

"It's the tobacco, sir. Gets over everything."

"Yeah, sure. May 17th, 1921." He looked up at me. "That'll make you nineteen?"

"Yes, sir."

"Don't call me sir. Call me Sergeant. Okay then. Through that door, take off your clothes and wait to be called."

The physical was a breeze. I guess anyone who was standing up and not a moron was in. That night I slept in a London barracks, after a difficult long-distance phone call home. I prayed that Grandpa or Charlie would pick up the phone, but it was Gramma.

"Where *are* you?"

"London, Gramma. I just enlisted...Gramma? Hello? Are you there?"

"You can't enlist." Her voice was faint and the line was full of crackles and pops. "You're under age."

"It's okay," I shouted across the miles. "I'll write and explain. I'll send you my address."

I wanted to say "I love you, Gramma," but there were a dozen guys lined up for the phones, so I just rang off and went to my barracks, feeling a bit ashamed of myself.

The bed was hard, with stiff blankets that smelled of disinfectant, and it took me a while to get to sleep. Around me I could hear other recruits moving restlessly, maybe with the same thoughts, a mixture of fear, regret and excitement.

We were given basic uniform with no flashes, and fatigues. We spent most of the time in those fatigues, painting buildings and peeling potatoes, marking time until one day when I was put on the train to Chatham, with a bunch of other guys, all of us heading off into the unknown.

I listened to the clickety-clack of the wheels over the steel rails and watched the countryside flash past the window. Suddenly I saw a kid sitting on a fence by the right-of-way, waving like mad. It might have been me, ten years earlier, sitting on the fence at Cornell, longing to be on the train.

As I waved back I thought triumphantly: *I've made it. I'm on the train.*

NINE

Dear Nance: I wish I had the time to sit down and write you the long letter that's going on in my head, but I just don't know when that'll ever be. As you know from my last, we've been down at Chatham for nearly eight weeks, after being issued with our uniform and basic equipment.

First were all the inoculations. We got sick, but do you think that held things up for a moment! Pause for a laugh. We drilled and marched and did push-ups and jumping jacks. When we were trembling with exhaustion they let us lie on our stomachs at the rifle range and learn to shoot straight.

Apart from the fact that we don't have two minutes to ourselves from reveille to lights out, it's not bad. The cooking isn't a patch on Gramma's, of course, but the food's eatable and there's always plenty for seconds.

I've met up with two guys from the Woodstock area. One is Pete Haines; his Dad has the feed store, remember! The other's Alex Baker. He's a tough little Scot whose father farms just south of Woodstock. I wonder if your folks know them! We've become good friends and Pete, who likes reading almost as much as you and I do, calls us "The Three Musketeers." All we need now, he says, to make life really interesting, is to meet up with D'Artagnan. As far as I'm concerned life is quite full enough already, what with reveille at 5:30, shower, shave, bed making, breakfast, inspection, march, drill, rifle practice, dinner, more of the same in the afternoon, followed by supper and instruction movies. By the end of the day we're too tired for mischief.

We fall into bed at lights out and before you know it there's that damn — sorry, Nance — that darn bugle again.

I composed that letter, and many others like it, as we marched to and fro across southwestern Ontario in full battle gear with packsacks, gas mask cases, helmets, rifles, and pouches at our waist for ammo and grenades, though we hadn't yet been issued with any such dangerous weapons.

I suppose I must have walked at least as many miles a day in my solitary explorations around Norwich, but then it was always with the knowledge that as soon as I had had enough I could go home to Gramma's stew and fruit pie and the comfort of my feather bed. And peace and quiet.

Now there was army food and a pallet that must have been stuffed with straw, and the knowledge that before I could relax and enjoy my well-earned rest I would have to scrape the mud off my boots, wash my putties, polish the brass on my uniform, and above all clean my rifle.

It was, at first, a bit of a let down. None of my adventure stories had hinted that the army might be like this. A couple of times, when I got really homesick, I was tempted to go to the C.O. and tell him I'd lied about my age and wanted out. But of course I never did. It was just a thought — a kind of escape hatch. I had to hang on and prove I could do it. After all, as soon as training was over we'd be shipped off to England and into the scrap. That's what I told myself.

After eight weeks at Chatham they shipped us up to

Borden and we got nine weeks of the same, only more so. We learned how to read maps so we could find our way around strange country without getting lost. How to recognize good places to fight from, and how to know the obviously bad ones, like being down in a swamp with the enemy on high ground above you. We learned a lot of ways of killing a human being, with rifles and automatic weapons, with grenades and bayonets, and in hand-to-hand fighting.

"Do you think you could?" I asked Alex one day when we were on kitchen fatigue.

"Do what?"

"Kill a guy with your bare hands?"

"Sure, if it was him or me. And so could you, laddie, and don't you forget it." He wagged his potato peeler at me.

"I don't know if I could." I still felt uneasy.

"Jerry's not going to sit around politely waiting for you to make up your mind to it. Would you rather be home with Granny the now?"

"No. No, of course not." I flushed and looked around to make sure the others hadn't heard his remark. It was okay for Alex to tease me because we were buddies, but I wouldn't want it to get around that I was "Gramma's boy."

After we'd finished our advanced training we marked time for a bit. Then we began to get furlough, the last, we guessed, before going overseas. Mine came at the end of April, and I hitched a ride in a truck down to Waterloo and caught the Woodstock bus from there, and another down to Norwich.

I walked in the door with my duffle bag over my shoulder, and Gramma took one look at me and burst into tears.

"It's just because you look so grown-up all of a sudden. Oh, Blaine, how could you do it? How could you lie about your age?"

That was a tough one. I tried to look her straight in the face.

"I wanted to enlist, Gramma. It was the only way I could get in. I...I changed my birth certificate."

"Oh, Blaine!"

That was all she actually said, but I knew I'd hurt her. She had set such store by bringing me up straight and honest. She'd got out of the habit of church-going in the bad years, with nothing fit to wear and not a spare cent for the collection. But she was good through and through, and right now the look in her pale blue eyes made me feel like two cents worth of nothing. I tried to smile.

"Come on, Gramma, I'm fitter than a lot of guys the army's taking now. Why, some of them are so thin and wore out you wouldn't credit it. You've always fed me well, and farm work's made me strong. I *should* go."

"Hmm." She stared up at me. "And I suppose the fact that you've always been hankering for an adventure wouldn't have anything to do with this high-minded sacrifice, would it?"

I blushed. "Maybe a little."

"Oh, my, Blaine Williams, there's a lot of Lil's flightiness in you! But thank the good Lord it's balanced by your Dad's steadiness. You're a good boy. Make sure you stay that way, mind. Don't do anything you'd be ashamed to tell me about."

"I promise." I laughed and put an end to the awkward moment by picking her up and giving her such a hug that she squealed for mercy's sake to put her down before I broke every rib in her body.

Then Grandpa came in from the barn, let out a shout

when he saw me and punched me between the shoulder blades the way he used to when I was little. Then he took his hand back and looked at it in a surprised way.

"Guess army life suits you, son."

"Except for the food, Grandpa. What's for supper, Gramma?"

The first thing I'd promised myself I'd do on this furlough was to go down to Tillsonburg and visit Dad. I caught the bus down and went to his rooming house. Like everyone else he was doing better financially, but he still had that ghostly look I remembered. What had caused it? I wondered. Was it losing the farm? Or Mom's desertion? Or was it something more like rust, something slow and insidious, growing from some small spot of weakness until the whole frame was eaten up by it?

Around Dad I felt suddenly too large, too loud, too assertive. It wasn't that he wasn't glad to see me. I could tell he was pleased that I'd come, though he didn't say anything — I wouldn't have expected him to.

I'd picked a Sunday, phoning ahead so he'd be expecting me, hoping we could have a whole day together. It was a fine morning and we walked out of Tillsonburg, though we seemed to have nothing to really *say* to each other. Oh, I talked about the army, and I told him about Pete Haines and Alex Baker. He smiled faintly when I told him we called ourselves "The Three Musketeers," but he hardly said a word. After a time I got tired of the sound of my own voice and we walked on in silence.

At length we stopped at a bridge over a little brook.

"Any good fishing hereabouts?" I asked, suddenly remembering his one passion.

His face brightened. "You'll get some lovely little Dolly Vardens out of here. Would you like to try?"

"What, now?"

"It was just an idea." His face closed.

"Dad, it'd be *great*. I just never thought about it. Have you got a spare rod?"

"Are you sure you'd like to...? It was just an..."

"Come on." I took his arm and hustled him back to his rooming house. While he dug out his fishing gear I coaxed some sandwiches out of his landlady and promised her we'd be back with fresh trout for supper.

Two hours later we were sitting side by side in a patch of sun watching our lines. The water was brisk and peaty, but there were places in the lee of large rocks that Dad said were promising.

The silence was okay now. It was no longer awkward. If it wasn't for my uniform I could almost have forgotten about the war, it was all so peaceful down by the water.

"When are you off?" Dad asked after a while.

"They don't say, but soon, I think."

"Funny to think of you going to England. Where I came from. Not that I remember much. More like a dream."

"Tell me where to go — to visit relatives," I asked eagerly.

He shook his head. "There's no one."

"Well then, gravestones. Church records." I hadn't thought of it before, but now the idea really appealed to me.

He shook his head again and lapsed into silence. He never *had* talked about his childhood, I realized, not once. Whereas Grandpa and Gramma, not to mention all their friends, could be set off by a single question and would never stop. How odd, I thought. What terrible sadness must be hidden away inside that silent man, my father.

We caught four trout. That is to say that Dad caught three, and I saved my honour by catching the last, which had probably been waiting in line for Dad's hook and become impatient. While we were packing up Dad said suddenly, "I'm sorry I didn't give you a better life."

I looked up in surprise. His head was bent over the honey pail, packing wet moss around the fish, so I couldn't see his face.

"But, Dad, it was just fine."

His knuckles whitened around the handle of the pail, and I suddenly understood that he hadn't been saying he was sorry I hadn't had a good life, but that he was sorry it had not been *he* who had given it to me.

"It's okay, you know." I put my hands over his. "I love you, Dad."

We walked quickly back to the rooming house and the landlady fried the trout for our supper. Especially after army food that sweet trout cooked in farm-fresh butter tasted like heaven.

Dad walked me to the bus stop.

"I'm sorry about your mother too," he said abruptly, as if the words had been torn out of him. "When I look back I realize I never understood how she felt about things, not ever."

I just didn't know what to say. We had stopped at an intersection. Even on Sunday Tillsonburg was pretty lively now, with the war and all.

"Not sure I understand you either," he went on. "Going off to the war before you have to. Leaving your Grandpa and Gramma. You're sure you were happy?"

"Yes. Yes, of course I was. Only..." How could I tell him that *his* idea of happiness, which was things being on an even keel with no actual disasters, wasn't mine. I wanted to talk to him about that yearning for adventure I'd had ever since the day I'd squashed the penny on the line and begun to count freight cars for luck. But he was right. He wouldn't understand. So in the end all I said was, "I just had this feeling I ought to go."

We stopped at the bus depot and he looked up at me. Now I was almost a foot taller than he was.

"You hold your newborn son in your hands for the first time, and you wonder," he said. "But you never know. You can never even guess." His face twisted, but he got it under control and went on. "I'm proud of you, son, real proud. Good luck."

Then he shook hands and walked away fast, leaving me standing by the bus.

He shook hands, for God's sake. My Dad.

I'd intended to drop by Uncle Bob's and Aunt Mary's, of course, to say goodbye. But they asked me to dinner — all formal, with the good china. I knew they meant to show they were proud of me too, but it made me feel suddenly like a stranger.

John's squadron was stationed somewhere in Kent and I took the address from Aunt Mary, determined to look him up as soon as I landed. After all, England was so tiny I was bound to be able to meet up with him.

The rest of the furlough I spent with Nancy. It was the Easter holidays, luckily, so she wasn't in school most of the time.

"Though I'd have skipped if it hadn't been."

"Never! You're far too law-abiding."

"You'd be surprised."

We walked and biked. And talked and talked. After four months of the mindless physical life of the army it was marvellous to be able to share ideas and books again, to feel my mind working; and to feel free to say anything, anything at all, about myself and know that it was safe to do so.

By the end of my furlough I was beginning to think I must be every kind of idiot to go off to England, leaving Nancy to finish growing up without me. Maybe finding another special friend.

I didn't allow my mind to go further than that regret. After all, what could I do? I was not quite seventeen masquerading as nearly twenty, and the future was just a great big question mark. I'd no right to tie her down.

But on the other hand, my mind argued with itself as I lay awake in the suddenly too soft feather bed, if I said nothing, she'd never know just how important she was to me. There seemed to be no way out.

Then suddenly it was the last morning, and I said goodbye to Grandpa and Gramma, to Rose and Charlie, not to mention Uncle Bob and Aunt Mary and Bill, Peg and Liz, who happened to drop by just as I was on the point of leaving. Then I walked into Norwich to catch the Woodstock bus. They'd offered to drive me but I wanted to go alone.

Nancy was waiting for me at the bus depot. We only had about five minutes, as the goodbyes had taken so much longer than I'd thought.

"I'm sorry I'm late."

"Don't be. It was a lovely two weeks."

"I'm going to miss you."

"Me too."

"You'll have all the other guys in Third Form."

"And you'll have all those beautiful English girls."

We looked helplessly at each other, neither of us saying what we wanted to. What the heck, I thought, and I caught hold of her and gave her a real kiss. She gave it right back. No doubt about it at all. I drew back and looked at her. The green eyes looked extra large, but a little smile twitched the corner of her mouth. I hugged her.

"Promise to write?"

"Of course. And you. If you can. I do understand it may be difficult."

"Time to get aboard, son," said the driver.

"Here. This is for you." She pushed a small box into my hand.

"But..."

"Go on. Get aboard. You don't want to be AWOL, do you?"

I picked up my duffle bag and climbed aboard. Every passenger's eyes were on me. As I found a seat they turned from me to Nancy, standing just below the window. It was a sunny day and she was wearing a pale green cotton dress with a white collar. She looked like home and love and security all rolled into one. I felt like a heel and an idiot.

Last term the English teacher had read our class an old poem by a guy called Lovelace, titled *To Lucasta, Going to the Wars*. It wasn't a success. His name broke up the guys right off, and by the last verse we were just holding our sides. Now, unexpectedly, the last two lines jumped into my head:

I could not love thee, dear, so much,
Loved I not honour more.

I found myself thinking that the teacher had got it all wrong, that honour had nothing to do with it and the poem was really an alibi. I just bet that Lovelace, in spite of his corny name, was longing for the adventure of war, running like mad from home and love and security, just the way I was.

The bus jerked and began to pull out of the depot. I waved and Nancy waved back. Then we were out of town and heading along the road to Waterloo. In the privacy of my hands I undid the little parcel. Inside was a small maroon case. Inside that was a wristwatch. A real beauty. Remembering how Nance's mother never gave her a cent for extras out of the egg money I wondered what she'd gone without to give me this splendid gift. Or maybe she'd robbed a bank.

I found myself smiling at the absurdity of the idea, and a lost memory tugged at my mind. I fastened the strap around my wrist and remembered. The trip to Norwich with Dad to buy school clothes. Dad had sold his watch and I'd been scared he'd robbed a bank. Full circle — and how lucky I was.

There was a note folded into a spill shape inside the maroon case. I unfolded it.

Dear Blaine: I wanted to get you something that we could share as a remembrance. There's five hours difference between us and Greenwich Mean Time, so we won't be doing things at the same time. But whenever I look at a clock I'll be thinking of you, five hours further on. Take care of yourself.
Love, Nance.

I put the note carefully into the box and buttoned it into the breast pocket of my battle blouse. Then I looked at the time. I looked at it quite often on the trip back to Borden.

We're still here, Nance, I wrote two weeks later. *Cutting the grass and raking the paths and repainting the white posts and chains that stop people walking on all the nice grass we've just cut. Is this what we enlisted for? Your watch keeps great time. I just wish the days wouldn't go by so slowly.*

Finally about twenty-five of us were mustered and sent off by train to Halifax. We were to be replacements, we were told, in the Second Division in England. Seems the Essex Scottish were under strength and we were to bring them up again.

"Replacements for what?" Pete remarked, after we'd been given our orders. "The Second Division hasn't *been* anywhere."

"Och, they've probably died of boredom." Alex rolled his r's with relish. "Mark my words, laddies. That'll be our fate too."

Looking back I think Alex must have been some sort of a prophet; but the move itself was exciting. I never let on to the others just how I felt as we climbed on the train.

Halifax was a brawling crowded exciting city. We were lined up and marched first here and then there, and at last we found ourselves aboard a passenger liner, part of a convoy assembled for the perilous journey across the North Atlantic.

I looked at that great grey mass of heaving water, going on and on forever, meeting the sky at some place I could barely see, and I was terrified, though I went on joking with the others and never let on.

We were packed tightly enough in the cabins, but it wasn't like a troop ship. There was room to move around and even exercise on deck, though we were warned that if we showed a light after dark we'd first of all be court-martialled and then thrown overboard.

Though we never said anything about it, I, for one, used to lie awake after we had bunked down, listening to the thrum of the engines and wondering if I might wake up with a torpedo amidships and the cold Atlantic coming in. It was a spooky feeling. But in fact we had an entirely uneventful voyage, apart from Pete's seasickness, which was bad enough to keep him in sickbay for most of the voyage. We were sorry for him, thankful that it wasn't us, and glad of the extra room in the cabin. I even got used to the vastness of the sea after the first couple of days.

It was a small convoy, and fast, so it was only ten days after leaving Halifax that we steamed up the Clyde to Grennock, a grey port on a grey day, that seemed to be inhabited by tired, grey-looking people. We were given travel warrants and put on a train to London.

At Euston there was more waiting, until at last a truck — the guy in charge called it a lorry — turned up, the twenty-five of us piled into the back of it and we lurched off across London. The bits we saw, past the tailgate of the lorry, were a real mess. We'd heard about the bombing, of course, but I hadn't really understood what it would be like. There were gaps everywhere, half houses with the stairs just hanging in space. A single wall standing, with the wallpaper of each room making a pattern. A wash basin on the second floor, still attached to the wall. The streets were gritty with brickdust and concrete; but the people seemed to be going about as if nothing was wrong, and gangs were cheerfully cleaning up the mess and putting hoardings around the deepest holes, so kids wouldn't fall in, I guessed. It was only later I understood what it was like walking around in the blackout.

The lorry left the city and the suburbs behind and then we were in the green countryside, but only for a minute or two. Every few miles we'd slow down and wind through another town or village. I couldn't believe people living that closely together.

We stopped finally at this huge army base southwest of London — Aldershot. I'll tell you, it was a darn sight drearier than Camp Borden, and I hadn't considered *that* was paradise. Everything was grey and muddy, and it kept raining, on and off, which would account for the brilliant fields and woods we had passed. Not that there was anything green about Aldershot. It was *all* mud.

We reported in and were signed onto the strength, picked up our gear and were sent off to our barracks. The drizzle had turned into a downpour. We trudged off with the water dripping off us, getting colder and colder by the minute, wondering if the sun ever shone here.

I pushed open the barracks door and the very first person I saw was Jim Aitken from Cornell, who'd befriended me at school and carved a boat for me.

"Jim, you old so-and-so," I yelled. Then I saw the two stripes on his sleeve. "Corporal Aitken! Blaine Williams reporting for duty." Then I introduced Pete and Alex; and Jim introduced us to the other guys. They were from all over Western Ontario, but two of them, Steve Graham and Mike Hall, were from Tillsonburg and remembered John from the flying days.

"We tried to get into the Air Force too, but they decided our feet were safer on pavement than on the rudder," Mike grinned.

"John's doing okay," Steve added. "Quite the old man. Got hitched last month."

So John had married! That was news to me, though once my mail caught up with me I would have all the family gossip from Gramma.

"What's it like here?" I asked eagerly. "And when do we move?"

"Ruddy awful. Well, you've seen the barracks. The food's worse."

"Worst of all is nothing to do," added Mike.

My face fell. Was it going to be like Borden all over again?

"Cheer up, kid. By the time you're as old as us maybe something will have happened. We've been stuck here since 1940, and they still haven't found anything for us to do except march up and down hills and freeze our butts off in these rotten awful billets."

Steve and Mike were right. Once we got settled, boredom crept in. Deadening leaden boredom. Marching and drilling. And in our off time nothing to do but go into town and get drunk and raise Cain. A lot of the guys did that. Sometimes there were as many men on report as there were men to guard them and march them off to the hoosegow.

Then at last we left Aldershot for Sussex. The Second Division was supposed to guard the Sussex coast against invasion; but, though being billeted in farm houses or under canvas was better than those awful barracks, it was still pretty depressing.

I had imagined writing brave letters home — we had all been so sure that by now the War Office would start a second front. Instead my letters got shorter and shorter. I mean how many times can you describe a forced march? The only person I really enjoyed writing to was Nancy, and her letters back became the high points of my week and mail call the best moment of the day.

Reading her letters was like walking beside her and listening to her talk; I'd find myself answering as if we were really together. I wrote back page after page, nothing about the boredom or guys coming in drunk and trying to break up the place. No, in our letters we walked right out of that summer of 1941 and into a private world outside time.

In July we got a break. At parade one morning we were told: "All men with farming experience step forward."

As I stepped forward, along with Alex and Jim and a

few others, I wondered what this could have to do with the war. Next thing we were in the back of a lorry bowling across the countryside.

Someone in the War Office had decided that since there was nothing for us to do we might as well help with the harvest. It was a marvellous month, going out every morning to some little farm. We worked our butts off, but it was like a holiday. The fields were tiny, surrounded by hedges and ditches, and you wouldn't believe the yield, forty-five bushels to the acre at least.

We stripped off our battle blouses and worked, from field to field and farm to farm, right across southern England, until the grain was all sacked and sent off by railway to be ground into bread for the hungry people of Britain. It felt good working with the sun on my back and the smell of ripe wheat and the scratch of the chaff. When we said goodbye to our farmer friends and headed back to join the rest of the regiment, guarding the Sussex Downs against an invisible enemy, it was like going back to prison.

The officers tried to keep us busy with forced marches, but as often as not they ended up as pub crawls, from village to village, with many of the men staggering into camp the worse for wear and on charges next day. Over the peaceful downs, where whole areas had been torn to pieces by transport and tank treads, we had battle drill, using live ammo and chucking grenades about.

Winter came and it was back to those awful barracks at Aldershot. It was cold and raining a lot of the time, and many of the men came down with pneumonia. Alex and Jim and I were lucky. That month of soaking up the sun while we got in the harvest had set us up ahead of the others.

In December we got the news of Pearl Harbour. The United States was in the war at last. But would the

Yanks be coming over to Europe or fighting the war in the Pacific? There were rumours everywhere. Then the Second Division got a new commander and slowly things began to look brighter, with younger officers in charge of the brigades, men who'd been trained and really knew what they were doing.

At Christmas I got a seventy-two hour pass and, at John's invitation, went over to the little cottage where he and Anne were living close to the air base in northern Kent. But it wasn't a success. John was different. It wasn't just the uniform or him being an officer, though he certainly looked both handsome and successful. But he was tense and jumpy and snapped at Anne a couple of times in front of me. I'd have guessed that he had been drinking, but he didn't touch a drop the whole time I was there. They weren't supposed to, Anne said, not when they were flying.

Anne was small and neatly made with short dark hair and a quiet voice, not the sort of girl to have attracted John, I would have thought. She was very kind to me, almost self-consciously hospitable; and very English, though I could hardly blame her for that. But the whole weekend was like a scene from a play, not real at all.

The cottage was the kind I'd seen in movies about England, with a tiny front garden, a white fence and a white gate and crazy paving up to the front door, where the lintel was so low I had to duck. Inside it was the same, all nooks and tiny cupboards and windowseats, diamond-paned windows and a brick fireplace. The chairs and chesterfield were covered with flowery material and the short window drapes were flowered too. It had a mixture of cosy charm and shabbiness completely different from your basic Ontario farmhouse. No matter how shabby it might be I knew that there would always be tea at four with good cups and sherry before dinner.

Inside this nest John's anger and nervous energy ripped and sent sparks off everything. Within twenty-four hours I found I was about ready to snap right back. I don't know how Anne stood it, and I felt sorry for her, the new wife, probably wondering if this awful John was the real one and what had happened to the cheerful young man she'd married.

She hinted as much the second afternoon, Christmas afternoon, when John was out.

"You've known him all your life, haven't you, Blaine?"

"Sure. Well, almost. Since I moved from Cornell to live on my Grandpa's farm outside Norwich." She smiled briefly at my pronunciation; in England it's called 'Norridge.' "He's always been my best friend," I went on. "As close as a brother, a kind and thoughtful brother, with no family rivalry, you know. He's changed a lot."

"You see that too? Oh, Blaine, I'm so worried. That's why I wanted to meet you, why I persuaded John — you're the only person I could talk to without seeming...disloyal."

"Is it his nerves?"

"I think so. My guess is that you can only go on so long pretending it's a game, like knights in armour having duels — do you know what I mean?"

I stared at her. That was *exactly* how John had originally thought about fighting.

"You do understand what I mean, don't you?"

"Oh, yes. He once said something exactly like that."

"I thought I was right. You see, after a time, with his friends gone — his closest friend Matt bought it last month — and when he'd shot down his tenth or twentieth Jerry and seen him go down in flames or into the Channel, well, I think it's stopped being a game anymore and it's become bloody and brutal. I think John is hating himself because of what he has to do."

"And *that's* why he acts as if he hates you half the time?"

"Yes. I don't mind it. Well, actually, of course I do. But it's all right. I understand why it's happening. But I'm frightened for him. If he's hating himself like this his judgment's going to be off some day. He'll make a mistake."

What could I say? I mumbled something and jumped up to help her tidy away the tea things. Then John came in with a couple of brother officers and the afternoon turned into a party.

The new year came and went. We began to work even harder at our practice war, marching as much as two hundred and fifty miles in eleven days. It was March then, the March of 1942, and there were golden buttercups all over the downs, and drifts of bluebells and primroses in the woods.

Soon, we told each other. *It's got to happen soon.*

TEN

It finally happened. On the day after my eighteenth birthday, my twenty-first according to my doctored birth certificate and my army records, we were told to pack up and muster. There was a short train ride to Portsmouth and then a ferry boat to this little island off the south coast, called the Isle of Wight. W.I.G.H.T., not W.H.I.T.E., the way I thought it was spelled with all those chalk cliffs.

Once we disembarked at Ryde there was the usual hanging about. I'd found out in the last year that the army was ten per cent marching and ninety per cent boredom. We loaded up all the heavy equipment into lorries, then marched twenty miles or so to a place called Freshwater. There, up above the cliffs were all these Bell tents, just waiting for us to put up and move into.

The first thing we got after we'd settled in was a lecture on security. Not a murmur about where we were or what we were doing, not even any guessing out loud. So for a while I was just writing to Nancy in my head again.

Dear Nance:
  It's a pretty little island, the sort of place where I guess people would take the kids for the summer. Right now only the permanent inhabitants are allowed to stay, and the island is sewn up tight. No one on. No one off. It's swarming with thousands of Cana-

dian soldiers and almost as many navy types. It's got to be the invasion!

Sometimes, while we're running up beaches strewn with live mines hidden just under the surface, and clambering up gorges filled with barbed wire, I imagine what it must have been like before the war, with families picnicking in the little coves, making sandcastles on these beaches, hanging their wet bathing suits out of the windows of the empty hotels and boarding houses. It's a crazy world, Nance.

As you know, I'm not crazy about heights, after Dad scared me off that time I climbed to the peak of the barn, so you'd really be surprised at me now, shinning up cliffs on ropes, crossing rivers in a breeches buoy, twirling on a rope above a river like a dumb beetle.

It's the toughest training we've had yet. The part I've just told you about is fun. It gives you a special feeling, Nance, to see just how far you can push your body. Once in a while, when I'm dangling from a rope, I suddenly find myself remembering Scaramouche or The Prisoner of Zenda, with the hero swinging from the chandelier. Then I nearly fall off, wanting to laugh at it all.

The other part of training isn't so hot. If I were really writing this letter to you I don't think I'd tell you about it. That's the learning how to kill and kill fast and quietly. Oh, we've done it before, but now it's becoming real. When Sergeant Blakeney yells at us to twist those bayonets in the sandbags I know that pretty soon it could be a real human belly I'm twisting my bayonet in. Could I do it?

We're learning to fire not just rifles but Sten guns from the hip as we run towards a position. These Sten guns are pretty bad. The magazines jam all the time and the firing mechanism could be better.

We each have our own gun and we spend quite a bit of our spare time filing them down and adjusting them until they're smooth enough to feel safe. I sure wouldn't want to go into action with a semi-automatic that was liable to jam. It'd be like fighting with your hands tied behind your back.

Even in my imaginary letters to Nancy I didn't tell her just how tough those five weeks really were. The problem was that we'd been hanging around so long that we'd gone soft. It wasn't too bad for guys like Pete and Alex and myself, but for those who had come over with the Second Division in the Christmas of 1940, well, they'd been waiting for something to happen for a year and a half. They'd already peaked and begun to go down.

Every morning we'd roll out of our blankets, line up at the mess tent for breakfast, and then be on the road with our packs, masks, helmets, grenades, rifles, the lot, all in all about sixty pounds weight. Then we'd march fast along the country roads that criss-crossed the island. Eleven miles in two hours flat. The second hour was pure torture.

When our feet were so swollen that it was tough to get out of our boots, and our legs were aching and our backs about to cave in, then there was street fighting through mock-up towns, like movie sets, and up green hills at top speed, or attacking concrete pillboxes with smoke bombs and flame throwers. Or they might give us more weapons training. It's tough to hit a target when you're so bushed the sweat's running into your eyes and you can't stop your hands from shaking. I used to think there was nothing like haying, back in the days with no equipment, for sheer hard work, but it was a picnic compared with combat training on the Isle of Wight.

"Remember suckering tobacco?" Jim Aitken said

one day, just trying to cheer us up. But even with a breaking back I'd say suckering was easier.

When we finally did that eleven miles in under two hours, our Battalion C.O., Lieutenant-Colonel McKay talked to us.

"Well done, men. That's certainly got some of the fat off us." He could honestly say "us," which was more than some of the officers could, because he'd marched every mile at our head; and if our feet hurt, his must have been every bit as sore.

"Now comes the real work," he went on. There was a bit of a groan, not enough to be a discipline problem, just enough to make him smile. "Now we take to the boats," he said.

My heart jumped and I thought: *This is it. We're off.* But of course it wasn't that. We were far too green. It was just more practice. Getting into landing craft, heading out to sea and then coming back in again as if we were making a landing in France. They made it as realistic as they could, with explosives attached to underwater wires, so that as soon as our landing craft touched them they went off and we came into shore with this fearful racket and water spouting everywhere.

The infantry landing craft — LCI in Army talk — were like flat metal barges, and we had to keep our heads down as we came in, because some sadists out there fired machine gun bursts right over where our heads would be if we *were* foolish enough to stick them out. As a result we couldn't see a thing, and since some of the navy types who were steering the landing craft had never handled such odd boats before, we got into a real mess. One time we finished up beached the wrong way round. The ramp went down and out we ran, yelling and cheering, only to find ourselves in water up to our necks, staring out to sea. It took us quite a while to get our Sten guns dried out and cleaned after that little mistake.

After a lot of practice at coming in altogether onto the right beach at the right time, all facing the right way round, we had to charge up the beaches while mortar bombs were fired just ahead of us, and top marksmen — at least we always hoped they were good — fired just in front of our feet so the sand kicked up at us.

Once I got used to all the noise and turmoil I found it was pretty exciting. The six of us were a unit. We sat together in the landing craft. We ran up the beaches together, firing from our hips at the non-existent enemy skulking in the brush that filled the gorges. Helping each other, we all grew pretty good.

Then we had to learn to swim, stripped or in full battle gear, with Mae Wests or without. That determined me never to swim in full gear. I'd sooner strip. As soon as the water got into that heavy wool cloth we'd sink like stones even without our boots.

By the time the C.O. was through with us, our battalion could run up nine hundred foot hills, scale cliffs three hundred feet high, land in any cove or on any beach on the island in complete silence in the dark, and disembark in about eight seconds flat.

"Good show, men. Now we're going to try a full-scale dress rehearsal."

Well, you know what they say about dress rehearsals. We chugged west for hours in those cramped LCIs. By the time we finally headed in to a stony beach in Dorset with cliffs looming behind it I was beginning to think we must be on our way back to Canada.

Then the ramp went down and we clattered up the beach, the pebbles making the darnedest noise you ever heard in the dawn silence. Yes, the silence. We got to the top of the beach and looked around. There wasn't a soul around except us men, a couple of sergeants and a junior officer.

"If this is an invasion I don't think much of it," I whispered to Alex.

"Och, me neither. Let's go away home to our beds."

The sergeant whipped around quick, but we were all standing there dumbly, waiting to be told what to do next. The officer struggled with a map and a tiny flashlight.

"Must be the wrong beach," he said at last. "We're too far west. Back to the landing craft, men."

There's a surprise, I thought, as we all trailed back.

By the time we got to the right beach it was all over. We arrived just after the tank landing craft, and *they* were an hour and a half late. We heard that the top brass, who'd driven down from London to see the fun, were furious. Our officers looked pretty tight-lipped about it too. As for us, we got back into those little boats and headed back to the Isle of Wight for a hot meal. And about time too.

We learned something from the fiasco, though. Apart from the difficulty of navigating the LCI's and getting them to the right beach on time, we found out that the Sten guns were a real menace. We had to do a lot more work on them to make sure they wouldn't jam in action.

We hung around the island for a whole week, with no leave and our mail heavily censored. Every morning we'd wake up thinking: *This is it.* The Fusiliers Mont-Royal, the Sixth Brigade, were busy teaching elementary French to us English Canadians. Some of the men were serious about it, but most just wanted to learn how to talk to the French girls.

A week later we had a second rehearsal. Apparently it went much better. But guess whose landing craft got lost again? Right. The Essex Scottish. We began to think we were jinxed. At least we didn't land at the wrong beach this time, but we were sure late coming in.

Then the word got around that we were off. The air was electric, like an August day in Western Ontario in tornado weather. There was that edgy feeling, the tingle under one's skin. Then at the end of the week the whole thing went flat with yet another exercise, this time using large infantry ships, with the familiar landing craft swung out in davits, ready to drop into the water. There were ships everywhere, destroyers, gunboats, radar ships, torpedo boats, tank landing craft. This was a full-scale affair and no mistake.

Then, in the afternoon, the gangway was swung aside so that the ship was cut off from shore. Our C.O. turned to us and said, "All right, men. This is it. The real thing. *Not* an exercise!"

Well, you couldn't hear him for the cheering. He had to wait for the noise to die down before he could go on.

"Shortly after midnight we'll set sail for France. Our target is the port of Dieppe."

After we had a meal we were told exactly what we had to do, and then it was just a question of waiting. I'd never seen a summer sky take so long to darken. But at last the stars began to come out and the moon rose, though it was hidden most of the time by fast scudding clouds. When it did shine you could see white flecks on the water, where the wind was blowing spray off the tops of waves.

The night dragged on. We dozed and woke and dozed again. The last time I woke there was a grey dawn outside. We were still lying in the waters to the north of the Isle of Wight. The expedition was called off. Tired, cold and flat, we disembarked and went back to our life under canvas on the high ground behind

Freshwater. There'd been an unexpected weather warning and the whole exercise had been cancelled.

After all we'd been through to get trained up to invasion pitch, we were sent back to the mainland to continue guarding the coast of Sussex against a Nazi invasion that we believed was never going to come. We were warned to say no word about where we'd been or what we'd been doing.

The first week of August I got another seventy-two hours, so I hitched a ride into Guildford and another to Maidstone, and a third to the cottage where John and Anne were living.

"You're looking fit," was the first thing John said as he opened the little blue-painted door.

"Should be. I've sure been working at it."

"Yeah." John took my duffle bag and dumped it on the bed in the spare room. "Heard about your show," he said under his breath. "Don't say anything to Anne."

Just then she called from the living room.

"I expect you boys would like a beer before dinner. I'll be about half an hour."

She gave us beer cold out of the fridge, so that the bottles were sweating, the Canadian way. I never could understand why the English liked their beer warm.

"Here's to us." I lifted my glass.

"I've got a special toast, Blaine. To Anne and the new addition to our family."

"Hey, that's great. Congratulations!" So that's why John didn't want a hint of the Dieppe invasion to get to Anne. He didn't want her upset.

"When's the baby due?" I asked.

"Next January. Mid January."

"That's really great," I said again. I looked at the two of them, sitting together on the chintz-covered chesterfield, the tiny diamond panes behind them, hollyhocks pink and wine-coloured nodding in the breeze outside.

Just for a moment I felt a twinge of envy for John. Then I thought: *Hey, that's crazy. See a bit of the world first. Have some adventures. You're only eighteen, Blaine Williams. Lots of time for all this.*

Anne jumped up to check the vegetables, and John and I caught up on family news, comparing letters from Aunt Mary with those from Gramma. I could see that John had worked through whatever it was that had been bugging him. He seemed very calm and happy, and whenever he looked at Anne he just glowed.

"Happy?"

"Yeah. I wasn't much company last time you were here, Blaine. Sorry about that. Had a lot on my mind."

"But you sorted it out?"

"Yeah. Thanks to Anne."

After supper, with Anne doing imaginative things to baked beans and spam and fried bread, the phone rang. John listened and put the phone down.

"Damn, I have to go. Sorry, darling." He slipped on his jacket, grabbed his hat, kissed Anne and ducked out of the low door. "Back soon."

"See you," I yelled after him.

I turned from the door to see Anne staring out, her fingers knotting and intertwining until I thought she would break them. I put my hands over hers. She buried her face in my shoulder, just for a second. Then she drew back.

"Sorry. Help me with the washing up, will you, Blaine? Then I'll put on a kettle for tea."

Halfway through the dishes she stopped, her hands in the soapy water, her head up, listening. Overhead I could hear the whine of fighter planes, Spitfires. Then Anne went on washing, rinsing and handing the plates and forks to me to dry.

"It must be tough," I ventured.

"Tough?" She rinsed the sink and dried her hands slowly. "Sometimes I think I'd rather not have met John. I had a very calm ordinary sort of life, you know. Secretary to a solicitor in Guildford. Do you know Guildford?"

"I've been through it. It's very old, isn't it?"

"Yes. Very old."

"What's a solicitor?"

"Oh, you'd say a lawyer, I suppose. Not one that pleads cases in court, though." She sighed. "I didn't really mean that, about wishing John and I hadn't met. I die every time he goes up, well, we all do, of course, we Air Force wives. But if I think of not knowing him, loving him, having his baby — well, I just can't imagine it."

The kettle boiled and she rinsed the pot carefully and made tea.

"Don't tell John"

"Tell him...?"

"That I worry."

The two of them, I thought, *trying to protect each other from that reality out there.*

We sat for hours in the slow English twilight drinking innumerable cups of tea. After a time Anne got up and made a fresh pot.

"I hope you don't mind if I don't turn on the light yet. I hate having to close the windows and pull the blackout curtains, and we have to be so careful here. They fly over us on the way to London, you see."

"I like it. It's restful. It reminds me of the days before we had electricity, back at Cornell."

She asked me about my childhood and I talked a little, but I could tell that she wasn't really listening. The travelling clock on the mantelpiece chimed nine. Then ten.

"They *must* have got back. It's quite dark now."

"There's debriefing, isn't there?" I guessed. "Maybe it's taking longer than usual."

"He always phones. Always."

A car scrunched on the crushed stones of the lane outside.

"There," I said. The relief was enormous. A car door slammed.

"It's not his car." She was across the room and had the door open before I'd even felt her move. I got up and stood behind her. The man wasn't John.

"Is he...?" Her words were out while he was still fumbling with the gate.

He looked up. "Yes, Anne. I'm so sorry."

"Definite or maybe?"

"Quite definite. Over the coast. Two of us saw him go down in the Channel."

"Thank you for coming, Nick." Her voice was flat and polite, very English. He came in and she shut the door behind him, closed the windows and secured the blackout behind the flowery drapes. Then she switched on the light. We blinked at each other.

"Oh, Nick, this is Blaine Williams, John's cousin from Ontario. Blaine, this is Nick Leewood, John's Squadron Leader."

We shook hands.

"Nick's from Port Arthur, Blaine. That's Ontario too, isn't it? Maybe you know each other." She took glasses from the corner cabinet and a decanter.

We gave each other a guarded look.

"It's a long way away. Ontario's very large. My grandparents have the farm next to John's," I told the squadron leader.

Then my voice suddenly wavered. The liquor Anne was pouring splashed onto the table. "Let me." Nick took the glasses from her and handed them out.

"Safe flights," he toasted, as we raised our glasses.

"And happy landings," Anne responded.

I took a long swig of straight Scotch that brought tears to my eyes and made my throat scream. Were they crazy, these people, with their "safe landings?" John was *gone*. I wanted to run out into the darkness, to race across the fields and scream at the sky, at fate, at the Nazis. At God, if he was listening.

Nick had found out from Anne that I was spending my leave at the cottage.

"Then you'll be all right? Or would you rather come over and stay with Rachel and me? She'd love to have you, you know that."

"No, thank you. I'll be fine. Blaine'll look after me."

They put their glasses down and shook hands, like strangers at a party. But at the door, before she turned out the light, he kissed her cheek and she clung to him. Then she switched off the light, opened the door and let him out.

When the light came on again she leaned against the door, looking white and drawn. Suddenly I remembered the baby.

"Shouldn't you be in bed? Would you like me to send for the doctor? I could phone."

She managed a smile.

"No, I'm fine. But I thought...oh, Blaine, his parents ..."

"Would you like me to write to them? I could do it now, if you like, and mail it in the morning."

"Would you? Thank you very much. Tell them I'll write soon. The first post goes at eight. If you wouldn't mind dropping it in the pillar box tonight. It's at the bottom of the street." She brought me paper, pen, envelope, stamps.

"I think I'll turn in now. Is there anything else you need?" I shook my head. "Then I'll be off. Blaine, I'm glad you're here."

I stared at the paper, screwing and unscrewing the top of the pen. I wrote a few lines, crumpled up the sheet, threw it in the waste basket and started over. After the third attempt I remembered that there was a paper shortage over here as well as a shortage of everything else, so I made the next draft do. I finished the letter "...they seemed so happy together, especially with the baby on the way."

I put on the stamps, switched off the light and went out, leaving the front door ajar. The moon had set and it was extraordinarily dark. A very long way off, towards London, a couple of searchlights wavered across the sky and then went out. I groped my way down the lane to the street and found what Anne called the "pillar box" and mailed the letter to Uncle Bob and Aunt Mary. Then I found my way back to the cottage and went in and closed the door.

It took a long time to go to sleep. Actually I wasn't really trying. I just lay on my back with my arm behind my head remembering John. All the good times we had had together. All the things we would never do again. Never even talk about again.

I woke to the smell of coffee and bacon. Canadian bacon. Anne was in the little kitchen when I went in. I kissed her, a little awkwardly, but she seemed to like it.

"You've got seventy-two hours, haven't you, Blaine?"

"Yes, but of course I don't have to stay if you..."

"I phoned the vicar this morning. The memorial service will be tomorrow. I'd be awfully grateful if you'd stay. And perhaps you could help me pack."

"Pack?"

"There isn't much that's ours. The cottage was only a billet, you see. I can't stay on here alone. Someone else will need it."

"Where will you go?"

"Home to Guildford. To my parents."

"Do they know? Would you like me to...?"

"Thank you. It's all right. I phoned them this morning."

I looked at the china clock on the windowsill of the kitchen. It was just five after nine. Anne had been busy. Dry-eyed and businesslike.

There were visitors all day, from the base and from the village. Sitting quietly in the background, getting up only to be introduced or to make fresh tea, I put together a picture of my cousin John, the Spitfire pilot, a man of puckish humour, reckless yet steady, a good friend.

When everyone had gone and we were cleaning up I said, "Anne, let's go out for dinner."

She looked surprised, then she said, "All right. Why not?"

We got a bus into Maidstone and found a restaurant. The food wasn't that great, but I felt it was a good idea to get her out of the cottage. At least I got her to eat a little.

Next morning I helped her pack. There wasn't much. Clothes. A few souvenirs and photographs. But among John's belongings was a model airplane that I'd made for him one Christmas out of a kit, when I was twelve or so. I'd completely forgotten it, but John hadn't. He'd even brought it to England with him. Kept it all this time.

I put my head down on my knees and cried. Then I was ashamed of myself, with Anne being so brave. But she put her arm around me and cried too. Maybe it was for the best, because up till then she hadn't shed a tear.

"Take it," she said. "As a remembrance."

"May I really? Don't you want...?"

"I don't need it, Blaine. I've got so many memories."

In the end I got her to hold on to it for me. It was a fragile thing, that would have been wrecked in my duffle bag.

Anne went to wash and change and I tidied up a bit and we walked down to the village for the memorial service. The sun was shining. Flowers grew in the long grass around the tilting gravestones, and there was a wistaria vine growing over the lich-gate in the wall around the old stone church.

Inside, though, it was dark with dingy-looking banners, and the vicar was very old and mumbled. I couldn't wait to get out into the sunshine again. One of John's friends commandeered a car, and we piled Anne's boxes and bags into the back and sat together in the front for the drive to Guildford.

Squashed beside me, I felt Anne turn to look at the cottage as we drove by, but she said nothing and sat staring straight ahead for the rest of the journey, while the Flight-Lieutenant gave me a guided tour of Kent and Surrey as he drove.

When we got to Anne's house I helped unload her belongings and shook hands with John's friend. Anne's parents came to the door, and there were more introductions and invitations to tea.

"No, I don't think I will, thanks a lot. I have to get back tonight."

"You must visit us later, when you have leave again. Please. I mean it. I'm sorry it was such a rotten holiday for you."

"Oh Anne!" I gave her a hug and a kiss and left. I went to look at the Norman castle and thought about eight hundred years of armies protecting this island against invaders. Eight hundred, nine, more if you think about the Romans and the Saxons and the Picts and Scots. Maybe that's why they were the way they were, so well-behaved and stiff-upper-lip.

I looked at a lot of other old buildings, and then I made my way to the Portsmouth Chichester Road and hitched a couple of rides back to base.

ELEVEN

On Tuesday, August 18th, we were suddenly told to get our full battle gear together. Then we were bundled into lorries and driven down in convoy to Southampton.

"Another stupid exercise," was Jim's opinion.

"Maybe this time it'll be the real thing."

"Blaine, you're a hopeless dreamer. Bet you a week's pay we're off to the Island again."

At the docks we mustered by companies and waited. And waited. Finally we were marched onto a couple of little ships, the *Prince Charles* and the *Prince Leopold*. We got the *Leopold* — what a name! As we were herded below decks I saw the familiar LCIs swinging from the davits. Well, at least now it's August the water should be a bit warmer, I thought.

At four o'clock Lieutenant-Colonel McKay stood up in the crowded mess.

"Well, this is it, boys. No turning back this time. Next stop Dieppe."

After the first cheer there was no time for celebration. As we began to break out our gear we found that the idiots in stores had sent us boxes and boxes of new Sten guns, straight from the factory, still in their packing grease.

"Why the hell couldn't they have let us keep our own guns? We'd just about got them ready to fire without jamming."

"These are bloody useless. How are we going to fight with them?"

Our platoon leader looked kind of white. I guess officer training had never prepared him for this kind of stupidity.

"We'll just have to spend the night cleaning them and adjusting them."

"Without firing them? Kind of difficult," Alex grumbled.

At least we weren't as badly off as one of the other battalions. It seems that some of the men, fed up with all these practice invasions, had dumped the ammo back at base and carried aboard dozens of empty boxes. They weren't laughing now. Nor were their officers. Lieutenant-Colonel McKay went to the captain and begged and borrowed every gun and spare bit of ammo from ship's stores.

And that wasn't the last of what went wrong. Whoever had loaded the machine gun belts had forgotten to insert tracer bullets. This meant that the soldiers firing them would have no idea if they were aiming correctly. What a way to start an invasion, I thought, even a little one. That evening in the crowded ship was an exercise in controlled panic.

"Wonder what else can go wrong?" Steve asked gloomily.

"Maybe it's like the rehearsal. When we get there it'll go like clockwork," I suggested hopefully. My stomach was like a leaden lump, and I hoped I wouldn't disgrace myself. I got permission to go up on deck for a breather.

We had just cast off. It was 9:30 by Nancy's watch. Five hours difference...or would it be six with double summer time? It would be late afternoon and she'd be helping her Mom cook supper. Around us was the shadowy bulk of other ships. As I watched, the sailors hoisted canvas superstructures and false funnels to make us look like an innocent merchant convoy, heading out of Southampton Water. In case of spies? That made me think a bit. Suppose they were waiting for us when we got to Dieppe? The whole point of the landing was that it should be a surprise. But suppose it wasn't?

I swallowed my panic and took a deep breath. It was a warm evening, the sky clear, the last rosy light of the sun reflecting off the downs. It had been a peaceful twilight much like this three weeks before, when John had gone down in the Channel somewhere east of here.

I went below. I needed companionship. We ate sandwiches and dozed a bit, or lay thinking of what the morning was going to bring, going over in our heads everything we were supposed to do.

At three o'clock on the morning of the 19th, that cold hour when your blood runs slow and your brain feels empty and courage has fled, we went up on deck and got into the landing craft. It was still very calm, with the sea just breathing a little, silky looking with the light of the setting moon dancing on it.

Packed like sardines, thirty or so of us to a craft, we squatted on the benches. Steve and Mike were over in the centre nearest the ramp; and Jim, Alex, Pete and I were against the metal bulwark on the left. We sat silently, not moving, though now and then you could catch the flash of a man's eyes. Someone dropped a tin mug on the iron deck and it was like a bomb going off. We all jumped and swore.

"Watch it, you careless oaf!"

Ahead of us Motor Launch 291 chugged fussily along, showing us the way to Red Beach, the left half of the crescent lying immediately below the town of Dieppe, while to our right other launches were leading in the assault landing craft with the Hamilton Light Infantry aboard.

I stuck my head up and took a quick look. It was just like the photographs we'd been shown. There were the long moles of the harbour running out to sea to the east, and the white mass of the Casino to the west. As we got closer the cliffs on either side of the city looked more imposing. Could they be climbed? The Royal Regiment and the South Saskatchewans and the Cameron Highlanders should be up there by now, putting the guns on the headlands out of action. Without their help we guys coming in on the open beaches would be sitting ducks.

I ducked as the destroyers behind us began to barrage the shoreline. The shells whistled overhead and burst in clouds of dust and smoke among the buildings across the esplanade.

5:10 a.m. Every moment our landing craft crept closer. By now we'd forgotten the chill and the wet spray and the early morning miseries. We were ready and raring to go. Now the east headland was wreathed in white smoke. Flames spat from exploding cannon as Hurricanes swooped low ahead of us. The naval salvos from behind burst in clouds of red and orange, and flak and tracers criss-crossed the clear dawn sky.

We stood up and yelled. This was exciting! Then sudden spouts of water shot up around us and fell like rain on our shoulders. The air was bitter with the smell of cordite. I heard a sudden patter like hail on the water and a cry of pain from the assault craft next to us. Shrapnel! We ducked down and crouched against the comparative safety of the bulwarks. That was *us* they were shooting at!

Three hundred yards off shore. Crouched, ready to go as soon as the ramp slammed down. I clutched my Sten gun so hard my fingers went numb. I let go and flexed them and tried to relax, to breathe slowly and evenly, pretending this was just another exercise.

Three red Verey lights suddenly lit the sky. The Hurricanes peeled off and headed back to England. The bombardment of the destroyers was turned off as suddenly as a door slamming. What was going on? Two hundred yards still to go and the only sound was the pounding of the shore guns at our tiny craft. This wasn't what we'd been told was to happen.

A hundred yards to go. Next to me Jim Aitken swore on and on in a monotonous undertone.

"The bastards. They've left us in the lurch. The bastards..."

The mortars in the bow of the landing craft lobbed smoke bombs along the shoreline. Our LCI nosed in to the beach. 5:20 a.m. on the button. For the first time we'd done it perfectly. The ramp swung down and there, ahead of us, was the shore of occupied France.

Steve and Mike charged ahead of me to the right. I saw them land and begin to run. Pete and Alex were directly in front of me. I leapt down the ramp behind them, thinking: *Today is for you, John.* And I tripped and went full length. Pete and Alex had thrown themselves flat on the beach and I'd fallen over them.

"Come on, you idiots," I tugged at Alex's shoulder. "Don't stop here. Get up to the seawall."

Everything seemed to slow down as Alex rolled onto his back. His eyes were glazed, staring at the sky. Pete was dead too. Pete and Alex. All along the beach, wherever the landing craft had beached, men were dropping.

I ran, or tried to run, and sprawled flat again. This wasn't just a pebble beach like the one in Dorset. These shingles were as big as your hand and they were smooth and round and they slithered against each other so your feet couldn't get a grip.

From up on the eastern headland the shells pounded down. Somewhere across the esplanade I heard machine gun and rifle fire. A ricochet broke a pebble in two and the stone leaped up and cut my cheekbone just under my eye. The little sting of pain cleared my head and I got back on my feet and slithered and scrambled up the slope to the first row of barbed wire.

Someone had already thrown himself across its coils, and two more had died as they had crossed. I swallowed and then pounded over their dead backs and up the last steep slope to the seawall.

Crouching out of the line of fire I couldn't see a thing, but over to my right the pebbles were piled until they were only three feet below the top of the wall. I crawled over and peered across the esplanade. A bullet whined over my head and I dropped and pressed my face against the cold pebbles, sweating with fear.

But in that quick glimpse I had seen the barbed wire along the top of the sea wall, huge festoons of it, running right along the front from the Harbour to the Casino. I looked around for help. The Regiment was scattered along a thousand yards of beach, some of us under the safety of the seawall, others dead or pinned under fire on the beach itself.

Then, according to plan, the tank landing craft crunched onto the beach. Now things will go better, I told myself. They'll be able to get up onto the esplanade, and behind their firepower we can demolish the barbed wire and get into the town.

The sun had just risen. It was a clear beautiful day, just the kind of day we'd hoped for. The first tank trundled down the ramp, its guns angled up to direct its fire over the seawall at the hidden enemy. The second and third were right behind it. Before they'd even reached the crest of the beach their treads had been torn off by the merciless shingle. The first two were destroyed by fire from the headland. The third was stranded, but could still fire its guns.

Behind the tanks came more of the Essex Scottish, B company. It was dreadful to watch helplessly as they tried to run towards the shelter of the seawall, to see them spin and fall, or stagger blindly on with blood pouring from them.

"Come on, men!" Lieutenant-Colonel McKay yelled. "Let's get that bangalore torpedo up here. If we can just shove it through the barbed wire and blow it up, it's a short run across the esplanade."

We pushed the bangalore torpedo into the coils of wire and crouched while it blew. But when we scrambled over the wall we found that the torpedo was faulty. Only the first three feet of wire had gone. There was another three feet to get through. We fought at it with wirecutters and our bare hands, while all the time the hail of machine gun bullets and rifle fire from the far side of the esplanade cut us down.

Someone thudded onto my back and I fell onto the wire, unable to move.

"Get off me," I yelled. "Come on, you creep, move!" I managed to wriggle sideways and found myself face to face with Jim Aitken. His eyes were shut.

"Jim!" I wriggled slowly back to shelter, pulling him after me. His battle blouse caught on the wire and I tugged at it furiously. Lieutenant-Colonel McKay caught me by the leg and pulled me down.

"Not without Jim, sir," I yelled.

"He's dead, son. Can't you see? Come on. Get down."

Battered and bleeding, we crouched beneath the wall to get our breath. By now almost half the regiment was either dead or too badly wounded to fight. Some of us began going down the beach and hauling up to safety anyone who was still moving. Even then the bastards didn't leave us alone. Their fire raked the whole beach, and as often as not the wounded were brought to safety by those now almost as badly wounded.

Our Company Sergeant-Major finally got a bangalore torpedo to explode properly right inside the barbed wire. Through the gap he and fifteen men rushed across the esplanade and zigzagged to the houses on the far side.

The rest of us who were still mobile stood under the wall and fired incendiary grenades across their heads at the houses. One big building, with two chimneys, slap in the middle of the row, exploded into flames. We cheered and watched the men duck out of sight behind the houses. Faintly, above the constant din of cannon, we could hear the chatter of their Sten guns.

It seemed forever before they came running back, dodging the snipers across the esplanade and rolling over the seawall on top of us.

"Couldn't get far, sir. There's a lot of Jerry troops coming in to town by bus. They know we're here now and no mistake."

I leaned against the wall, my Sten gun at the ready, staring through the smoke and dust. My right hand was beginning to throb where I'd torn it on the barbed wire, and my eye was swollen from a flying stone, but not enough to spoil my aim.

I pinpointed a sniper up on the roof of a building over to the right and blazed away at him until my fool gun jammed. I threw it down in disgust and looked around for another. There was one, up on a drift of shingle only a few yards out into the open. The guy whose gun it had been was lying face down and it was still in his right hand. I figured it would take me about three seconds to nip up that shingle slope and grab the gun, and about two seconds to roll down to safety again.

The shingle slithered round my feet as I scrambled

up. I reached out and grabbed the gun with my right hand and rolled back down the slope, deafened by a nearby shell. But dammit, I didn't have the gun. I couldn't believe my stupidity. I stared up the slope, blinking a sudden dizziness out of my eyes. There it lay, with the dead guy's hand still on the butt and another hand grasping the barrel. Mine.

Dazedly I looked down at the sleeve of my battle blouse, at the awful mangled mess dangling from the cuff. I slithered down against the wall with a kind of croak. I guess the man next to me must have turned and seen what had happened, because the next thing I knew he was grabbing my arm and wrapping a tourniquet around it and yelling for a medic.

He saved my life, I guess. I was so dazed and surprised I think I'd have just sat there and peacefully bled to death. I never got a chance to thank him. I never saw him again. Whether he died on the way down to the boats or in the crimson sea, or whether he finished up in a POW camp I just don't know.

Things got muddled for a while. The next thing I was really sure of was lying on my back under the wall with the sun in my eyes, listening to someone moaning. It was an awful noise and I wanted to tell the guy to button up, but I was too tired.

"Hold on, son. Here's some morphine." That was Lieutenant-Colonel McKay's face floating over me. The moaning stopped and I realized that it must have been me.

There was a dogfight overhead. Hurricanes and Spitfires against the Luftwaffe. A lazy dance high up in this incredibly blue sky. Like seagulls. Or maybe pigeons...

I saw the pigeons swoop and soar between the rafters of the barn. One of them fell out of the sky. No, not a pigeon, a Spitfire. Down towards the sea, turning and twisting like a maple seed. John had finished like that. *Splat*. "Not a whole bone left in his body," Dad had said. I shut my eyes, but the picture of the ground coming closer and closer, twisting round and round, wouldn't go away.

Bam. Bam. The noise shook the beach. Mortar fire from the headlands, rifle fire and machine guns from the town and from the pillboxes on the esplanade. From our guys too, and the couple of tanks that were still operational. *Clatter, slash, shake.* "You've got to watch out," Mom had warned me. "You could lose an arm in that old thresher. What good would you be then? Without an arm?"

A mortar from the east headland hit one of the stranded tanks square on. It went up in a sheet of flame and billowing black smoke. The poor devils inside didn't stand a chance. Trapped. Like the chickens in the barn. Fool chickens clucking their heads off and running back into the flames. Grandpa never did find out how the fire started. A cigarette, he guessed. A careless cigarette from a farm hand. "A moment's stupidity and there's a year's work up in smoke."

Yes, Grandpa. I nodded. *A year's work. Or a life's ...*
Someone was shaking me.

"Huh?"

"If I help you, can you make it down to the landing craft?"

"Hell, yes." I shook the mist out of my eyes. "My legs are okay."

"Wait till I say, then, and we'll make a run for it."

I saw that it wasn't just the mistiness in my eyes. They'd put up a smokescreen along the shoreline to cover our retreat. Maybe it made sense, but it also signalled to the gunners up on the headlands what was happening. At once they turned their guns from the beach to pound the shoreline. You could tell exactly where the landing craft had come in. That's where all the bodies were. Lying at the edge of the sea, the tide reddening with Canadian blood.

"Now!"

His arm round my waist. My good arm over his shoulder. We pounded down that slithery slipping beach and I was dumped like a sack of wheat into a landing craft already packed with men, most of them wounded, some already dead, I think. I tried to thank my rescuer, but he'd turned back and was wading knee deep through the water, going back for another man.

The shells were landing in the sea on either side of us, sending up great salt water spouts. I could hear shrapnel spatter against the metal sides of our craft and I prayed we'd make it back to the assault ship without sinking.

I blacked out for a bit. The next thing I'm sure of was being on the deck of a ship. It was pitching and tossing, rolling from side to side like a porpoise. Turned out it wasn't an assault ship at all, but a destroyer that had nipped in and picked us out of our sinking landing craft. Our lucky day, I guess.

The pain was really bad. I could feel it down my arm and clean into my fingertips. I remember thinking: *That's crazy. I don't have any fingertips.*

Someone wiped the sweat off my face and gave me a sip of water. One of the seamen, I think. I could feel the heavy serge of his uniform against my cheek. And someone said — or was that later? I'm not sure — "How old are you, son? You don't look old enough to be fighting."

"I'm eighteen, sir," I said without thinking, being high on pain and morphine. "May 17th, 1924."

"Why the hell did you get into this mess if you didn't have to?"

"It was the train." I could hear my voice as if it were

a stranger's, a long way off, like an old-fashioned radio. "I thought I could get the train out of there. But I picked the wrong train."

"What d'you mean, son?"

"I thought it was the passenger train through to Detroit and Chicago. But was just the old Toonerville Trolley."

Blood all along the line, I thought. *Or were they just Grandpa's tomatoes for the canning factory?*

TWELVE

One last train. The right train this time. The train to Woodstock on the way back to Gramma and Grandpa. Back to the farm. Almost two years older. Travelling light, but with a load of memories, most of them the kind I wouldn't wish on my worst enemy. With two artificial army-issue hands to replace the flesh-and-blood one I'd left home with. One was a shiny brown leather affair, which hung awkwardly on the end of my arm, looking as if it would be more at home on a city fellow with a three-piece suit. The other was a business-like hook I was already pretty smart with.

Clickety-clack. The train swayed and lurched across the melting fields of an Ontario spring. I'd been in English hospitals right through the fall and winter of 1942. One thing after another. But now I was fit again, with a clean stump and no complaints.

At least being stuck on the sick list for so long had meant I was still in England when Anne's baby was born. In fact, they'd given me an overnight pass from the convalescent home to go to the christening.

It wasn't held in the little country church with the wistaria over the lich-gate, of course, but in a grand cathedral church in Guildford. Anne insisted that I should be one of the godparents.

"I can't hold the baby," I had protested. "I'll drop him for sure."

But Anne had laughed at my fears, and she was right.

I snuggled the little tyke into the crook of my left arm and managed just fine, even when it came to the time to name him: John Blaine Cameron.

Anne was making a new life for herself and her son, as widows all over Britain were learning to do. Across Canada too, I thought, remembering Dieppe. What a wicked waste! We'd been on that beach for only six hours; and of the Essex Scottish alone, only forty-one of us had got back to England. Of the rest, half were dead and half were prisoners-of-war. I'd lost every one of my buddies. Pete, Alex and Jim from the farm down at Cornell. Steve and Mike from Tillsonburg. The Musketeers had never found their D'Artagnan.

I shut my eyes against the memory of the loss. Perhaps the high-ups learned from all the dreadful mistakes. Perhaps when the *real* invasion of Europe began, they would do it better, because of our sacrifice. That's what I told myself.

Some day soon I was going to have to gather up my courage and visit their families. Tell them about their boys and the last hours we spent together on August 19th, 1942. I dreaded it. I knew I would feel their eyes on me. I knew what they'd be thinking. *Why should he have lived? Why Blaine Williams and not my boy?* Why not Pete? Why not Alex, or Mike or Steve? Why not Jim Aitken? I'd asked myself this same question a hundred times already, and I didn't have the least idea of the answer.

The other thing I was dreading was facing Nancy for the first time. I told myself I was crazy to worry. In her letters she had never faltered; they had kept me going in the very darkest days and lifted me out of all my self-centred wallowing. But face to face?

I told myself that I must give her a chance to get out. Not to feel obligated in any way. Not to stay with me out of pity. She had stood by me — I must be as fair to her. I hung onto these noble and high-minded thoughts as the train ran into Woodstock station.

"Need any help, soldier?" The conductor asked.

"No thanks. I'm fine." I swung my duffle bag onto my shoulder. It was light enough. A few mementoes. John's model plane.

As my feet hit the platform I took a deep breath. Even in the station the air was clear and tingly, with the smell of melting snow. I could hear water rushing along gutters and down spouts. Maple syrup weather.

I stood on the platform, wondering whether I should go straight to the bus depot and check the time of the next Norwich bus or whether I should visit Pete Haines' dad at his feed store and get it over with, or do what I really wanted to do, which was to find a quiet café somewhere and stop for a sandwich and a cup of good coffee. I was still standing there when she came flying out of the ticket office.

"You're early! How could you *do* this? I've been meeting every train this week and now I almost missed you because the train was early. The train's *never* early!"

"Nance!" I dropped my duffle bag and grabbed her in a hug; all my high-minded resolutions about being fair and giving her a chance to back out went clean out of my head.

After a while I drew back to let her catch her breath. Something had happened to Nancy in the time I'd been away. She'd had her hair cut for a start. Instead of two skinny braids there were now soft feathery curls, coppery brown. I touched them. They were like silk.

"Do you mind? Long hair was such a nuisance."

"I like it. It suits you."

The freckles were still there, a faint sprinkling

across cheekbones and nose, somehow making her skin look even clearer and fresher. Her large green eyes were...

"Hey, you're crying. Nance, what's the matter? There's nothing to cry about, is there?" I suddenly thought: *There's someone else.*

"It's okay, Blaine. I'm just so happy. And relieved. I wasn't sure what you'd be like. But you're still *you*, two years and a war away."

"Not quite the same." May as well get it over with now as later. I held up my right arm with the polished leather hand on the end. It never ceased to surprise me. I waited, cringing inside, for her reaction.

"Real high-class," she said, with a wicked imitation of Grandpa's voice. "Is it any good for cleaning out the barn?"

I laughed. "I've got a really good hook for that."

She looked into my face. "Then we don't have a single thing to worry about, do we?"

I took a deep thankful breath and kissed her hard.

"No, Nance, we don't. Not a thing." I picked up my duffle bag and we walked together out of Woodstock station. At that moment I wouldn't have traded places with the King and Queen.

We had lunch in a quiet little restaurant, and Nance told me how she had managed to borrow a friend's car and some probably illegal gas to come up to Woodstock and meet me.

"I wanted us to have some time together. Not to have to fuss about the bus."

"Some time? We've got all our lives, haven't we? Oh, gosh, I forgot. Nance, you will marry me, won't you?"

She laughed. "Of course I will, silly. Why do you think I've been staying at my girlfriend's in Woodstock all week, ever since we got your letter? So as to make sure of meeting you before you saw all those other Norwich girls."

"There never would have been another girl. Say, shall we go out and buy an engagement ring? I've got quite a bit of pay on me, and more to come."

"Don't you dare waste your money, Blaine Williams! Your Grandpa's talking about retiring in a year, now you're safely back. The farm'll be yours. We're going to have to save every penny to do over the house and maybe buy a few more cows."

"Yes, Nance." I looked across the table and grinned.

We talked and talked. Lunch turned into tea. At one point Nance excused herself. When she came back she said, "I just phoned your Grandma and warned her that we were on our way. So we have to be sure to be in time for supper."

"Oh, you shouldn't have. I was just going to turn up. No fuss."

"No *fuss*? My, Blaine Williams, you've still an awful lot to learn about women. Your Grandma's been counting the days. How is she ever going to let you know how much she loves you if you don't give her the chance to cook up a storm for you?"

So, just as the sun was setting and the evening star shining over by the farm, Nancy drove up the familiar lane. "You go in first. I'll just park this out of the way," she said tactfully.

I walked slowly past the front porch with its white painted pillars and the gingerbread trim under the eaves, along the side where I'd once sat all night in the old Buick and watched Grandpa's barn burn down.

I could smell hardwood smoke and the tangy scent of fresh maple sap. So I *was* in time for sugaring off. I pushed open the door to the summer porch and wiped my heavy army boots on the rag rug. Then I opened the kitchen door. The smell of fresh bread and pie and roast chicken came out to meet me.

Gramma and Grandpa were waiting. I looked at the two dearest people in my growing-up world, the people who'd given me a centredness, a security; and I wondered why I had ever wanted to turn my back on them, on the farm, on the daily patchwork of sugaring off and ploughing and seeding, of haying and threshing, of the daily rhythm of cows and chickens?

This, after all, was the place where I belonged, the place I would never again wish to leave. The train had lured me away with its false promises of money and excitement. But I'd been lucky. I'd been given a second chance. In Europe the boys enlisting after me would have to fight the Axis powers and clean up the mess. And there was still the war in the Pacific.

But right *would* prevail in the end, I told myself, so long as people didn't let themselves become complacent again, didn't let the evil take hold. We had to make sure that Dieppe and the rest wouldn't be completely wasted.

Nance slipped through the door behind me. I could feel her quiet presence at my side. We would have our own wars to fight, I knew that, small wars with hail and drought, with falling prices and quotas. With sickness and the raising of a family. Maybe even disagreeing over how to bring up our kids. But that was part of being alive too.

Then Gramma's arms were round me, and Grandpa was choking up and thumping my shoulder. I looked round the big old kitchen. Bigger than I remembered. It had always been full of people, but now Aunt Rose and Charlie had their own place, and Greatgramma had died at the age of ninety-six. I looked at the empty rocker by the stove and thought: *It's crazy, but I believe I'll actually miss the old witch!*

This big house needs people, I realized. Maybe I can persuade Dad to come back and live with us. Watch his grandchildren grow. Learn not to be afraid of living. There are many ghosts. Many memories. But maybe Nance can teach him...

...I'm almost at the end of the last tape, so I guess this is as good a place to stop as any, in the old farm kitchen with my sweetheart beside me and the future, full of promise, ahead of us.

So, Blaine, this is for you, as well as for my children and grandchildren, and the other great-grandchildren that may come along. But it's also for the gallant people who made it through the depression years, people like Gramma and Grandpa, Charlie and Rose and the vacuum salesman. And for the damaged ones who didn't quite make it, like Mom and Dad, though I think his last years with us were as happy as he dared let them be.

And it's in memory of cousin John and Jim Aitken, Pete and Alex, Steve and Mike, all the boys who never made it back from Dieppe and Normandy and Italy and the Far East. We truly believed that there was going to be peace, that what we had gone through was worth it; now it seems to me that greed was the winner, greed and fear.

Just don't forget that greed leads to suffering: like my dream of the New York Central — of escaping to the big city with its stores and lights — turning into the nightmare of the Toonerville Trolley, the Grim Reaper. Blood all along the line.

But there's always the freedom to change, to be better. And now it's yours, my grandchildren, and yours, young Blaine, the first of the next generation. It's in your hands to make this a better world. God bless you...